SHOESTRING

by Richard Leito Sentieri ⋯ ⋯⋯ved.

Gist

It festers deep down inside the pith of our being. Like lava that succumbs to the pressure of the Earth's core, it's trying to burst out. Trying to force its' way to the surface. Our desires and aspirations bubble up from our subconscious. It spews out into reality. What we do and what we leave behind reveals who we have become. Follow your inner compass and choose wisely. Choices are like footsteps walking down the thorn full path of life.

Breaking News!

Deep in the northern woodlands a new day begins. Under the sullen gray sky, snowflakes swirl in the wind. Whips of smoke drift up from the chimneys of rustic cottages that are nestled around a frozen inland lake.

Along the lakeshore amongst tall evergreens, hidden within twisted thicket, three wolves sniff the air. Out on the lake a fawn carefully steps across the glassy plane of ice. A crackling sound from underneath spooks the fawn. The deer's tail twitches while searching for food. It hops further out onto the lake. Creeping close behind the frighten animal the wolves follow.

On the other side of the lakeshore someone dressed in a blaze orange snowsuit scrapes the sidewalk with a snow shovel. He takes a break admiring the Christmas lights blinking on the quaint grocery store. A few doors down the baker turns on the "Yes we're open" neon sign.

Passing by, a large yellow snowplow truck pushes the snow down the street. On the corner several pedestrians wearing snow-pants and winter jackets wait for the traffic light to change.

With a scarf wrapped around their face a pair of eyes watches as the traffic goes by.

Muffled by the thick scarf the woman says, "Even with this blizzard, look how busy Lakeshore Drive is."

Feeling cozy inside the furry lined apparel, a man replies, "It's happening all over again."

After the snowplow drives by the light changes. The pedestrians then cautiously maneuver across the slippery asphalt roadway.

Hoisting a leather bag over his shoulder, the man says, "You know where we're going for breakfast?"

The woman looks at the man and replies, "Norma Gene's Early Bird's Special is the best deal in town."

The two then continue to walk past a large snowman. Entering the diner, the man holds the door open for the woman and they walk inside.

Inside the busy eatery clinking silverware mingles with light morning conversation. Mouthwatering scents of maple syrup, bacon and hot buttered biscuits fill the air.

The man helps the woman with her coat and hangs it up. Wearing work cloths, blue uniforms and identification badges, they wait to be seated. A petite waitress, wearing a brown uniform with a black apron wave to them. Wearing heavy steel-toed work boots they walk across the black and white checkered floor. When they reach the counter, they sit down in the last two remaining seats.

Clearing away the dirty plates off the white laminated countertop the waitress greets them.

"Well if it isn't Martha, and her husband Gildardo. The hardest working couple in Moon Lake."

Martha says, "We worked twelve hours last night and we're tired and hungry." Looking around the diner Martha adds, "Patricia why is it so busy?"

With a Spanish accent, Gildardo jokingly interjects, "Is breakfast free today?"

Trying to be discrete Patricia leans closer and whispers, "Bounty hunters and news reporters."

Speaking softly Martha replies, "I know everyone's talking about it."

Gildardo vainly strokes his greasy short black hair, "They say a strangler is on the loose."

Tapping her order pad with the pencil, Patricia says, "The usual, two chorizo omelets, green-chili and double order of tortillas?"

The young couple replies with an agreeing nod as the waitress jots down the order. Patricia then rips the order off the pad and sticks it on a small carousel that hangs between counter and kitchen area. She then brings the couple clean silverware and pours them two glasses of water. The waitress then asks them if they need anything else before she speeds away to service other customers.

Sitting there, Martha and Gildardo realize how everyone in the diner is transfixed, watching a television news report. On TV, a female wearing black denim jeans and a black wool sweater, holds a microphone that has the number six on it.

The news reporter brushes back her auburn hair as a chill runs down her spine, "Hello, I am Vicky Markus for Channel Six News. Welcome to our broadcast live from inside the infamous Unicorn Theater. Ever since it was rumored to be built on an ancient Indian burial site, this theater has been in the spotlight. And, it was here a decade ago where seven people were found dismembered. A few days after this horrific discovery, the theater mysteriously burned to the ground. But as we all know the story does not stop there. Soon afterwards, as a memorial to the seven victims, the community of Moon Lake rebuilt this classic theater from the ground up." Standing on a stage in front of theater's big white movie screen, she continues, "And, this afternoon, everyone will be gathering here for a remembrance service. After the service, the theater will then prepare for an event that has some reeling in disgust. The première of the movie, 'Shoestring Strangler' will be shown here tonight. This movie is based on a book written by Dean Stein. Mr. Stein was employed as the janitor of the theater when he was found here unconscious at the infamous bloody crime scene. The body of his wife, Janis Stein was one of the slain victims discovered. Stein, who was convicted for this crime served nine years before being cleared of all charges. While he was in prison, he penned the manuscript. What got him off death row? A DNA profile extracted from several pieces of evidence discovered at the Unicorn infamous crime scene. Earlier today, Taskforce Commander, Jack Mahoney said that they are waiting to see if the Unicorn DNA profile is a match to the DNA found at the Chicago murder scene of the nine-year-old, Jeffery Vaughn. The young boy's body was discovered strangled to death in an alleyway in Chicago last week. The body was dismembered just like the victims' bodies of the Unicorn Theater. Also, like the theater victims, a shoestring garrote was found neatly tied around the young boy's neck. The bloody alleyway was discovered by a homeless individual. FBI Agent Mahoney said that they do suspect that the results of the DNA test today 'will match the DNA recovered at the Unicorn Theater's crime scene'. There is also another disturbing fact about the Chicago murder victim. Jeffery Vaughn lived and grew up here in Moon Lake. The young boy was from the same neighborhood as the theater victims of ten years ago. But today is a big day for Moon Lake. A talent contest, snowmobile race and of course the huge movie première is scheduled. Stein, who has always stated that he was forced to sign a confession, has been busy promoting the book and movie. However, because of the detailed imagery of the novel, most readers firmly believe that Stein is the Shoestring Strangler. One positive aspect of the big movie première is that all the revenue from the movie will go to a victim's relief fund. This fund directly helps those who are affected by violent crimes. After the première, Mr. Stein is throwing a party at his lush mansion, Hanson Manor. However, who's on the guest list isn't the question on everyone's mind." Curiosity then fills the reporter's blue eyes. "The blaring question is. Who is the Shoestring Strangler? This question has Moon Lake residents horrified and this frayed community is just about to unravel. Most residents have already stocked up on supplies and are behind locked doors. However, the streets are not desolate. Moon Lake has become the most macabre tourist attraction the world has ever seen. East Lakeshore Drive is crawling with tourist. Because of today's remembrance service and aforementioned potential blockbuster movie première, all the hotels are booked solid. Friends and families of the victims to intrigued amateur sleuths have come from all over the world. Not to mention the international news media who are arriving here in busloads." Watching the newscast inside the diner, with hunger gripping his gut, Gildardo salivates anticipating a sweetly buttered, hot and crunchy tortilla.

He turns to his wife and says, "I can smell the tortillas."

In disbelief, Martha replies. "Did you hear what they are saying on the news? The Shoestring Strangler could be outside waiting for us."

Gildardo looks out the ice frosted window.

His mind trudges through the memories of how his wife, child and he had left their homeland. *I should have known by the smirk on his face. The man who we paid to help us to come to America was greedy liar. He laughed as he stabbed me in the gut and left us in the mountains to die. If it wasn't for Martha's idea to keep tortillas and a canteen of water, wrapped up in the blanket with our daughter, we might not be alive today.*

Rubbing the knife's scare on his belly, Gildardo looks at his wife and says defiantly, "I'm not afraid."

From out of the cacophony of conversations, an angered voice shouts, "Be quiet. I want to hear the news!"

On television, the attractive long-haired woman holding a microphone walks over to a tall, balding man wearing a dark suit and tie.

"Good morning and welcome back to our live broadcast from inside the Unicorn Theater. I'm Vicky Markus for Channel Six and joining me is the Mayor of Moon Lake, Theodore Whitaker." She looks up at the mayor, "With the killer still at large, are people safe?"

The reporter lifts the microphone up to a to the bespectacled man's mouth.

In an assuring tone of voice, he replies, "Yes, they are safe. The Moon Lake residents elected me for times like this." The stoic man pauses before he continues, "We are not in any danger. We are safe."

Concerned and using a sympathetic tone of voice the reporter says, "Many who are left wallowing in the wake of the Shoestring Strangler are exasperated. In the original investigation why were authorities so convinced that Stein was the killer? Was it because his wife was one of the victims?"

The Mayor shifts his weight, "As you know Dean is my nephew. Since his release he has donated money to the school and to our city's parks department. Dean also insisted for the premier to be shown here. This decision has generated needed money for our local businesses. Concerning the initial investigation, I have no comment. Except to say that the ones who conducted the investigation have passed away or have retired."

Trying to dig out some emotion from the mayor the reporter says, "The victims' families are in turmoil knowing that the killer has been on the loose for all these years. Will it be different this time around?"

The mayor replies, "Back then things were different. Equipped with today's advances in criminology, crime assessment tools are more efficient."

The camera shot fades into another view positioned in the theater's lobby. It focuses in on a, "We'll never forget" banner that is surrounded by flower arrangements.

Watching the television inside the noisy diner. A teary-eyed elderly couple sits in the booth along the ice frosted windows. Oblivious to everything around them they look into each other's eyes. The woman thinks to herself.

I have never known him to act this way. Drinking straight whiskey every day, doesn't eat or take his medication, what am I going to do? The woman looks at the man who is sitting across the table. *He has not touched the sunny side up eggs or the potato pancakes.*

She then says to him. "Do you want to go home?"

With a voice embedded with pain the man pushes his plate away. "Is this really happening?"

Comforting her broken partner, she gently pats his hand. "She's at peace."

Caring steamy plates of food away from the waitress station, Patricia looks at the couple. She is touched by their apparent sadness.

Walking from table to table filling up coffee cups the waitress thinks. *They look so sad. I wish there was something I could do. Their daughter was so sweet and talented. She could've been somebody.*

victim list

Outside the diner snow falls gingerly to the ground. Next-door to the diner, on the marquee of the Unicorn Theater the neon sign blinks, "Shoestring Strangler".

Nearby, on the street corner a paperboy shouts out, "Moon Lake Gazette. Come get your Moon Lake Gazette."

A woman wearing a green wool scarf stretched over her face walks up and buys a copy. She then walks into a bus shelter and sits on a bench. Her brown eyes peer over the scarf as she begins to read the newspapers' headline.

"Victim #8".

Reading the details about the tragic accounts of Jeffery Vaughn a wave of deep sadness engulfs her as she thinks. *Jeffery was just a kid. His freckled face and that goofy smile. Why would someone kill him? He was just a kid being a kid. Toilet papering houses and playing ding dong ditch. A lot of kids do stupid stuff like that.* She cringes as she continues to read the specifics of the killer's diabolical method. Her bottom lip quivers. *No one deserves to die like that.*

When she is finished reading the article, she turns to the special section that highlights the remembrance service. The pictures of the killer's victims are followed by brief biographies. Their smiling and dreamful eyes are a testament to their vitality. However, before she finishes reading the article a blue bus pulls up. Folding the paper up, she tucks it under her arm. She then steps in line with other people boarding the buss. When the door opens, the graying, dark-haired bus driver says, "Watch your step." After the woman gets on the bus, the man says politely, "Good morning Judy."

"Good morning Bill."

Wearing a navy-blue hat with an emblem of two mallard ducks flying over cattails, the man then says jokingly, "Yea, you're going home, and my shift just started."

Walking past the driver the woman sighs, "I'm beat."

Grimacing she adds, "My feet are killing me."

Along with the other passengers the woman finds and open seat. With everyone seated the bus continues on down the snowy street. The woman takes the scarf off, unties her fur brimmed hood and loosens the zipper from pinching her neck. She leans back in the bench seat and thinks.

I'm going to take a nap, have a glass of wine and then watch my soap. She then turns and looks out the window. Her mind relaxes watching snowflakes melt on the windowpane.

Trying not to be dragged into memories of past, she says, "Bill, are you going to see the movie tonight?"

Without taking his eyes off the road he replies, "No, I'm going to the lodge and have a couple of beers."

Trying to relieve the queasiness in her stomach, Judy takes her phone out and thumbs a text message.

This day can't end quick enough

After a moment a text comes back:

Don't let it get 2 you

She replies:

I LOVE U RICH! U always take care of me

IT's MY JOB! I'm your husband

Judy then closes her eyes and takes a slow deep breath. Haunting images of the past send shivers up her spine.

Whispering to herself, "Why did I go to clean the theater that night? It could've waited till the morning. And now, how can I ever forget what I saw. Those haunting images are etched into my mind!"

Driving past the iron gates of the cemetery, with the wheels crunching through the snow a young voice blurts. "Look! That's where they're all buried."

All the passengers except Judy turn their heads and gawk at the graveyard.

From the back of the bus someone adds, "Yep, all the Shoestring Strangler's victims are buried there. And people from all over come to visit those gravesites."

Standing up a woman points her gray mitten at Judy and exclaims, "Ask her, her husband works at the graveyard. She knows."

"Ms., please sit down." the bus driver scolds the boisterous passenger.

Driving through the falling snowflakes the bus becomes quiet. It remains silent until the breaks screech to make another stop. The door then swooshes open allowing passengers to get on and off the bus.

Across the aisle from Judy an elderly woman says, "How many Shoestring Strangler victims are there?"

Before anyone answers her the engine revs up and the bus continues to drive down the road.

With the windshield's wiper swiping back and forth, clearing the snowflakes from the bus's windshield, the driver answers.

"The killer is responsible for eight victims that we know of. Seven were found ten years ago inside the Unicorn Theater. And last week, the Shoestring Strangler killed a young boy in Chicago." Using the rearview mirror, the bus driver glances back at the woman. "All eight victims were born and raised here in Moon Lake."

The chatter in the bus increases as persistent blabbermouths fight for their voice to be heard. Realizing that she will not be able to relax, Judy reluctantly takes out the newspaper and tries to read it.

The overenthusiastic voices fade as she buries her nose deeper into the newsprint; *In a verified letter the Shoestring Strangler wrote; "Seven more will be murdered by eight PM tonight".*

Judy's imagination streaks and her light brown eyes widen. Gazing at photographs of the killer's victims her eyes stop at Janis.

We were like sisters. Judy's heart fills with sorrow remembering all the things they did together. *We did each other's hair, nails and make up. We were on a double date when she first kissed Dean. They were such a cute couple. Janis and Dean took it upon themselves to help everyone in the neighborhood. They went as far as to have the basement remodeled to include a bumper-pool table, pinball and video games for the neighborhood kids. Dean also sound proofed the garage so that the neighborhood musicians had a place practice. When the band learned a new song, they would play it for the whole neighborhood. Their cookouts and bonfires filled many summer nights.*

Again, Judy looks at Janis's photograph, deep into her shiny eyes as grief pricks at her heart. Combating her tears, she continues to read the article. The article begins with a short biography of Janis. The article goes on to state a summary of her life. It ends with the fact that she was killed at the young age of thirty-four.

The next two victims listed are John and Jason. Besides being in the neighborhood band, they worked with Judy at the Unicorn Theater.

The paper read; *No one ever did find out about their late-night poker games up in the projector room.*

Reminiscing, Judy continues to read about the other four victims. Jose and Emanuel Ramirez were also in the band. The twin boys grew up four houses away from Judy. It went on to state how they helped the elderly by doing yard work and shoveling snow.

The last two victims Judy reads about are Julie and Shannon. These two best friends were inseparable. They helped Janis make diner and deserts.

As she reads on, Judy reads about the latest victim. That Jeffery's family grew potatoes and that is how he got his nick name, Spuds.

Like he is reading her mind, the bus driver says, "Hey Jude, Spuds was so full of life. He always had a big smile on his face. I remember when it was snowy out and he'd wait for the bus to stop at a stop sign. Then, he'd sneak up behind it and latch onto the bumper. He'd hold on tight sliding on his belly down the snowy streets. Being deaf didn't hold him back. Spuds was a thrill seeker."

Judy puts the paper down and whispers depressingly, "Dam, he was just a kid."

Like a slap in the face her mind wakes up to a terrifying fact. The killer is still out there.

Stopping at a crossroad, the bus makes a turn and begins to drive along lakeshore.

The bus driver says, "I've been driving around Moon Lake for twenty-five years. Shuttling people around this lake has given me the opportunity to become friends with a lot of people. From watching them board the bus to go to school, to becoming adults. I watched a lot of them grow up to raise their own families."

Before the bus driver can elaborate his passengers talk over one another telling stories about the victims.

Blocking out the blabber mouths, the driver thinks about what Judy is going through.

Wishing he could say something to make her feel better, he looks at her in the rearview mirror. *She'll be okay, she's a tuff bird.*

To the beyond with love

Inside the gates of the Moon Lake Cemetery, footprints in the snow lead to the service door of a dark green garage. Inside, there is a large silver hearse and tools hanging on the walls. Sitting at a workbench a man wearing tan overalls, knitted hat and a winter jacket, takes a bite off a sandwich. Sunk behind distinguished pitted nostrils, his gray eyes squint as he chews on the chunk of liverwurst smashed between raw onions, cheese and bread.

The man says to himself, "I've been working here for all these years and have nothing to show for it."

He grimaces as he peels off a piece of the bread and tosses it on the floor. Almost instantly, a small brown mouse scurries out of the shadows and snatches the crust. Watching the rodent nibble on the bread, using his fingernail, the man picks at his teeth.

He picks up a clipboard, he studies it.

"What? They're filming a documentary on the killer's victims? Clean off headstones and put down some road salt? It's too cold to be cleaning headstones. Besides why can't folks just bury the dead and get on with their lives?"

Frustrated, he shoves his hands into insulated rawhide gloves and walks to the door.

"I guess I'll take a look to see how bad it is snowing."

Opening the door, the snow whips him in the face. Feeling the winter wind bite, he pulls his knitted hat down over his ears. Looking along the tree line that runs behind the shed, through the glistening ice covered branches he sees someone kneeling at a gravesite.

"There's Lexis Lynn. Knowing what she's been through, how can I complain about my situation? Her ma gets killed and her dad gets railroaded."

Kneeling at the foot of a snow-covered gravestone, a young woman unties and pulls down the hood of her black insulated snow suit. Wearing black leather boots and purple knitted gloves, she wipes the frozen snow off the grave marker's inscription.

As her big green eyes sheen over she whispers, "Janis Lynn, Loving Wife and Mother."

Tracing the stone carved inscription with her finger a tear wells and runs down her cheek. Taking in a deep breath of the sharp cold air, she thinks back to when she was a little girl. With snowflakes falling on her face, her flowing long blond hair whips in the wind, she reminisces. *I was seven and it was early morning, when the sun seems to be at its brightest. I heard a knock at the front door of the orphanage. I ran downstairs to answer it. I ran because my mind was still immersed in a dream where my parents had come to take me home. Even knowing that they had abandoned me, my arms ached to hug them both.*

She looks up to the snowy gray sky and in belief that her deceased mother can hear her thoughts.

The dream felt so real. And, I was so disappointed when I had opened the door and seen you and Dean standing there.

She then looks at the grave marker. *"I'm sorry mommy. I will try to forgive Dean. I know that he raised me as his own. You both were the best parents ever. And during the summer we would go to the lake and make sand castles. I will never forget the good times making chocolate chip cookies with you and going to the park with Dean. At night you'd read me a bedtime story. I can still here you sing. 'You are my sunshine, my only sunshine. You make me happy when skies are gray. You will never know dear how much I love you. Please don't take my sunshine away'."* Tenderly she then whispers. *"Mommy, I love you."*

Without warning the winter wind blows her hair off her shoulders. Trembling, she puts her hood back up over her head. Wiping away her tears brings the gravestone back into focus.

Submersing comfortably into her own reality, she says. "Mama, it's happening all over again. A note left by the killer said that more people are going to be killed at eight o'clock tonight. Don't worry about me Sandy is staying at our house. You remember her. Yea, she's the fortune teller who makes her own wine. She said that she's not leaving Moon Lake until this is all over. She came up here last night with her friend, Zongzi. He's a dream weaver. And he's cute. No Mama, I'm not trying to change the subject. Zongzi sings and plays harmonica. Sandy says he's a nice guy. I bet he already has someone. Besides, there's not too many men who want to start a family with an overweight thirty-one-year-old woman who's bipolar. That also takes prescribed psychotropic medications. Yes, I know love will find a way. Anyways, you know how clairvoyant Sandy is. Remember the tarot card reading Sandy gave me last time she visited? It said that I'm going to live a long life and have children. I'd like to believe her, but I don't see that happening."

Looking up at the snowflakes falling from the sky she sighs. She then looks back at the gravestone.

"Do you remember her wine making recipes? She says that her recipes allow your spirit to escape the flesh. Our life source is then free to breathe and be rejuvenated with no physical limitations. Yes, she's very spiritual. I knew you would remember. Well, Sandy has brought up two bottles. She thinks the wine will reveal who the killer is. Sandy said that tonight, Zongzi will drink her dandelion wine and be pulled into an all-knowing dreamscape. In this dreamscape, Sandy says that Zongzi will be able to see the truth. When he wakes up, he'll tell us who the killer is. I know, it does sound crazy. Okay mommy, I got to go now. If anyone asks, tell them that I'm doing just fine. I'd stay longer, but I'm meeting Sandy and Zongzi at the diner. Where's Zongzi staying? He's staying at the lodge and Sandy's staying with Patricia and me. Now, please don't worry mommy, I'll tell you all about it. And, I when I know for absolute certainly that Dean had nothing to do with the Shoestring Strangler. Then, he'll be my papa again. Mommy, remember that you're always in my heart and I will be back soon to visit you."

The young woman kisses her hand, pats the grave marker and stands up. Listening to the snow crunch under the soles of her boots, she walks past the tombstones of the killer's other victims.

With them in her thoughts she prays, "God please watch over my friends and their loved ones who miss them terribly. And through Your merciful love may we all find peace."

Driving out of the cemetery in her gold sports car she reminds herself about all the police officers who are looking for the killer.

She whispers, "I am carefree. Lungs breathe deep, free and focus on bringing tranquility into reality."

Instilling positive thoughts her eyes grow bight and she smiles. *It's a little nippy. Wow! Doesn't all this glistening snow on the tree's branches look amazing?*

Hopelessly in ruin

Peering out of the alleyway, from across the street, two pairs of bloodshot eyes move side to side. Wearing black wool masks that covers their head and ears, they try to conceal their identity.

Seemingly mesmerized by the distant tinkling of the little bell above the diner's door, one of them whispers, "There's Norma Gene's All-Night Diner. I love watching them come and go."

Not paying any attention to what is said the other person listens to a monotone voice coming from ear-buds.

"Let's liberate these treacherous unbelievers. Our righteous pilgrimage, guided from above it is time for another piece of the puzzle to be put in place."

The one wearing ear-buds, with snowflakes blowing into their face, takes out a gold coin and kisses it.

"It's a runaway freight train. By the time you hear it, it's too late to get out of the way."

The predator's pupils shrink to the size of a pin. Their twisted thoughts rattle down a crooked track. In an attempt to soothe shaky hands, reality is skewed. Anticipating sinister revelry, deep rooted impressions forsake morality. The tortured soul is flush. In vain purposeful thoughts surrender to oppressive unmanned voices that again come to life through ear-buds.

"It's time to take the trash out."

Griping a shoestring garrote, the immoral, self-serving defect rationalizes their diabolical plan.

Inside the diner, a group of the patrons sit at a table and wait for their meal. Looking around they admire the restaurant's old pictures showcased on knobby pine walls.

Pointing at an old black and white picture of settlers in front of a building, a woman says, "Isn't that the same place that's having the talent show?"

A man sitting at her table replies, "Look, this picture was taken 1881. It says that the Hunter's Lodge was one of the first buildings to be constructed up here in the northern woodlands. It also says that it was built using only timber logs and wooden nails."

Nearby, wiping off the counter, the waitress notices that Martha and Gildardo have finished their breakfast. She walks over to clear their dishes.

"How was everything?"

Martha smiles back at her. "Very Good Patricia. How do you say? Authentic."

"It tasted like grandma cooked it." Gildardo adds.

The waitress then says, "Thanks for coming and we'll see you next time."

Before the couple leaves, Gildardo peels out two dollars and places it on the counter. Standing outside of the diner, they are stunned to see so many people in their snowy little town. Gildardo then takes his wife by the hand and walks to the street corner.

Deeply troubled by all the hype concerning the slayings, Martha quivers and turns to her husband.

"I pray that little Marie and grandma are safe."

Gildardo replies. "We'll take the shortcut and get home quicker."

Waiting unsuspectingly in the alleyway across the street a demented mind grasps for purpose.

One of them whispers and point at the couple.

"That's them."

Looking down a crooked finger, adrenalin begins to ferment. Grinning, the fiend savors perverse images that fester up from deep within.

"Ah, they look so charming. Arm in arm drawn to destiny."

Walking toward the alleyway the young couple cross the street. Shielding herself from the windblown snow, Martha places her head on her husband's shoulder.

"Can't wait to be home to our family."

Gildardo responds by putting his arm around her, "I can wait to relax by the fireplace."

Martha quickly adds, "Going to feed little Marie, give her a bubble bath and then I'll join you."

The couple then walks into the alley. Watching them approach the stalkers' eyes widen in anticipation. Inside the fiendish mind, self-empowered, menacing voices tightens their bloodthirsty grip. Relinquished, lustful ambitions scoff at a deeply suppressed breath of morality. The invading impulse celebrates.

Purification awaits.

Succumbing to an irresistible, whimsical desire, lucid thoughts reach out of fantasy and forcibly take hold of the unsuspecting couple. The pouncing dreadful moment is fueled by their resistance. The use chloroform defuses their desperate struggle and it renders the young couple unconscious.

Collusion

A hawk glides against the snowy sky and sails over the church's bell tower. Inside the bell tower a police officer uses binoculars to search for disorder. Across the street on the windowsill of a large gray stone building pigeons coo and bob their heads. On the other side of the window, inside the building's conference room, dedicated professionals poke holes into theories. Spaced along the light green walls there are pictures of distinguished civil servants. With determined hearts and fixed eyes, a collection of law enforcement officers scramble to sit down at the tables that fill the room. Holding a vanilla folder, a lanky man wearing a dark blue suit walks in the room and toward the podium.

Standing behind the podium between two draping flags, the dark-skinned, silver haired man clears his throat.

"Hello, I'm Jack Mahoney."

The man takes off his coat and lays it over the back of a chair. A police officer who is sitting in the rear of room thinks.

For his age, he's looks to be in good shape. Let's see how he handles this.

At the podium, gazing over a crooked nose, that looks to have been broken several times, Jack scans the attentive assembly.

He takes a sip off a glass of water and says, "Let's start at the beginning. Most of us in this conference room realize an embarrassing fact: That it was within these same four walls, where Dean Stein was coerced into signing a bogus confession. It was the result of eighteen hours interrogation without food, water or bathroom breaks. Not only did they deprive Mr. Stein of his rights, they went as far to show him pictures of his wife's dismembered body. The intense interrogation pushed Mr. Stein into dramatically pounding this table with his fists as he shouted. 'Okay! I am the Shoestring Strangler!' After this admittance, the lead detective working on the case, finally allowed him to change his soiled trousers. As we know, Mr. Stein was formally charged and held without bail. And it didn't get any better for Mr. Stein. When the judge ruled that he could receive the death penalty, Mr. Stein made a deal with the District Attorney. If he agreed to plead guilty for the crimes, the DA would take the death penalty off the table. The following morning Mr. Stein calmly stated factual, in-depth, details of the morbid crime scene. These confidential details were enough to convince the District Attorney that they had their man. During the trial Stein was stoic. He displayed no remorse. He acted coy until the judge handed down a three-hundred-fifty-year jail sentence."

Jack pauses to take a drink of water.

"Reacting to the judge's decision, Mr. Stein came out of his fog. He exploded emotionally. While being dragged away by the bailiff, Mr. Stein vehemently proclaimed his innocence. As we all know he served nine years before undisputed DNA evidence proved his innocence. Now, we do sympathize with Mr. Stein and anyone who is falsely imprisoned. The fact is twenty-five percent of confessions are false. But that's not why we're here. We're here to protect the citizens of Moon Lake. It's our duty to uphold the law. Let's not be distracted by the media or any ballyhoo. We must remain focused. As you can see, we're under a microscope. So, let's get down to the facts."

Walking in front of a large media screen Jack points to a diagram of Moon Lake.

"All eight victims grew up in the same small neighborhood. And, profilers suggest that the perpetrator or perpetrators will continue to target these residents. The bloody crime scenes suggest a very personal motive. Profilers also believe that friends and family of the victims stand out as suspects. One thing is for sure whoever is responsible is highly intelligent and reserved. They do not stand out in a crowd. Oh yea, the note discovered in Chicago stated that seven more residents will die before eight o'clock tonight. We also have the results that the DNA recovered at the Chicago crime scene is a match to DNA recovered at the Unicorn Theater. Innocent lives are at risk. Residents of Moon Lake are being targeted. It is our duty to protect them."

Dream Detective

Hearing the bell above the door tinkle, Patricia turns around to see two people walk in the diner. After they take off their coats, the light skinned blond-haired woman and dark-longhaired man dust the snow off themselves.

The waitress walks behind the counter, puts the coffee pot down and goes over to greet them.

"Hi, Sandy, Lexis said that she'll be here soon."

Wearing a light blue turtle neck sweater, blue jeans and a purse in hand, Sandy replies, "Thanks Patricia. I love your apartment. Thanks for letting me stay with Lexis and you. That couch is like sleeping on a big marshmallow."

"That's good. Did I wake you up this morning when I broke that glass? I was pouring a glass of milk when it slipped out of my hand."

Sandy replies. "No, I slept like a rock."

Smiling at the man accompanying Sandy, Patricia says, "You must be Zongzi. I've heard stories about you."

Dressed in a black denim pants and a multi-colored tie-dye tee shirt, he replies, "The best thing about stories is that they all end and a new one begins."

Sandy then interjects, "With a killer on the loose why are so many people coming here?"

Patricia replies, "Don't worry Sandy, the diner is the safest place in town."

Looking at Sandy, Zongzi says, "With a killer on the loose, I should stay with you at Patricia's place."

"Zongzi, you're staying in the best room at the lodge." Sandy snaps back.

With snowflakes melting in their hair, they follow Patricia to an open table. Reaching the table, Sandy and Zongzi sit down.

Patricia looks at Sandy, "I've made more in tips this week than I did all of last year. I was going to work a double shift but I 'm going out tonight. Maybe we can hang out later." Before Sandy can reply the waitress adds, "Be right back to take your order."

Heading toward the kitchen doors, Patricia disappears into the busy diner

From outside, a lustful gaze looks through the frosted window of the diner. Their heavy breath fogs the window as a chill runs up Sandy's spine. Looking for the creepy vibe she calmly surveys the diner.

Sensing the presence of evil, Sandy looks at Zongzi, "Do you feel that?"

Looking through the slits of his bloodshot eyes, the unshaven man says, "No. This place is a circus. It's like the old west when people came from miles around to see a hanging."

Sandy digs in her purse, takes out a cell-phone and lays it on the table. She looks deep into the eyes of her friend.

"You look a little green around the gills."

With his face flush, Zongzi steadies himself by holding onto the table.

"It's the booze from last night. It's feels like sludge gurgling in my stomach."

Walking up, Patricia takes her order pad from out of the pocket of her apron.

Looking at Zongzi she says. "I hear that you play a kooky harmonica."

Wanting to lose himself in Patricia's soft eyes, Zongzi tries to smile.

"Yea kooky."

Sandy chuckles, "Patricia, as you can see, poor Zongzi's all played out. His last girlfriend left him passed out in his own vomit. So, he says that he's done with women because they use him like a Kleenex."

Interrupting the conversation, a patron in the diner calls for the waitress. Patricia acknowledges them by holding up her index finger.

Before walking away, Patricia leans closer to Sandy and whispers, "Do you think you could give me a tarot card reading?"

"I can do that." Sandy replies.

The waitress then waves bye on her way to service customers.

Sandy says. "She wants me to give her a reading. I wonder what her seventy-eight cards will say."

Coming back to the table and carrying a pitcher of water, Patricia says, "Ready to order?"

As the waitress pours them each a cup of ice-water, Sandy reads the menu.

Folding up the menu, she says, "Zongzi will have the pancakes. And I'll have some coffee."

"Anything to drink with the pancakes?" The waitress eyes Zongzi.

"I'd like gin on the rocks."

Before she walks away to turn in the order, the waitress smiles at Zongzi. "Okay, pancakes, coffee and a glass of water on the rocks."

Displeased by Zongzi gaping at the waitress, Sandy nudges him.

"Snap out of it. So, I suppose you're going to pull out your harmonica and make a big scene. Come on Zongzi, let's get focused."

Carrying a coffeepot and a plate of pancakes, Patricia walks back to their table. She places the plate in front of Zongzi and turns up a coffee cup for Sandy.

Zongzi smears butter on the pancakes while he watches the waitress pour Sandy some coffee.

When she is finished pouring the cup of steamy dark brown brew, Patricia smiles at Zongzi, "If you need any more syrup, just holler."

Patricia's voice invigorates Zongzi and he thinks out loud, "What a delightful vixen."

He then grins at the waitress and begins to eat pancakes.

Blinking her cat-like green eyes at Zongzi, the waitress says, "I think Lexis likes you. She told me you were named after a Chinese's recipe for rice dumpling. Is that true?"

Sandy interjects, "I think his name derived from his complete disconnection with reality."

"Yea, Lexis also mentioned that there is nothing normal about the Zong." the waitress jokingly adds before she walks back toward the kitchen.

Savoring the mouthful of pancakes and hot maple syrup, Zongzi leans back in his chair.

"I thought you admired my disconnection with reality."

Trying to change the subject, Sandy says, "How much sleep did you get last night?"

"Not much. I'd say, about three hours."

"Prefect, you should be out like a light right away. For our plan to work, everything has to be perfect."

"Sandy, is it going to work?"

"Zong, follow the path. Do what's natural. You can ask questions, but don't squander precious moments wondering about the answers. Don't get caught up in the big picture. Keep your momentum steady or you'll be caught up in a bog. Be filled with the power of love and be ready when you rise above the fog. Just relax."

"Do not be worried, I get it. For the clues surface, keep my mind in the glow. Go with the flow."

Sandy quickly responds. "No. Open your mind, tune in the flow and it will put you into the glow."

"Can you tell me where this journey going to take me?"

"The journey will take you through dreamscapes. If you stay focused, you will be able to seek out maniacal impressions that will reveal who the killer is."

"You had a premonition?"

"Yes, you're going to learn to be comfortable in your own skin."

"Will these dreamscapes cure this torturous hangover?"

"If you want to worry about something, worry about waking up without knowing who the killer is."

Zongzi sighs, "I hate to cut to the chase, but did you bring some of your homebrew with you?"

"Yep, I brought some of my best homebrew just for you. Two bottles of sweet dandelion wine. One to get yourself out of the way of yourself just in time. And the other bottle is an emergency backup. I also brought a bottle of sour green apple. You'll like it. It's to entice your spirit out of the dreamscape."

"Sandy, I got to level with you. Last night, I got drunk because I am scared out of my flipping mind. I just hope I don't piss or shit the bed."

Sandy looks deep into Zongzi's eyes, "I have complete confidence in you. I know that you don't remember most of your past dreamscapes. But you can do this. Your subconscious knows what to do. So, please don't think any more about it."

With both hands Zongzi rubs the self-doubt off his face.

"Anyways, thanks for bringing that sour green apple wine. That's some tasty spirits. It has an after-bite like a mule kick in the groin."

Patricia then comes back carrying a coffeepot. "Would you like some more coffee?"

"Yes please." Sandy requests.

Looking at the waitress Zongzi says. "These pancakes are gorgeous."

"Thanks, Zong, I'll tell Felipe the cook." Patricia giggles and then she attends to the other tables.

While servicing the table of several customers, she over hears their conversation.

A woman says, "He was drunk out of his mind. He said we're being invaded by aliens. Then he asked me out on a date."

A woman sitting across the table from her then says, "The mayor asked you out on a date?"

Ignoring their conversation, Patricia says cheerfully, "How's everything?"

A balding man with a gray moustache and goatee, replies, "The potato pancakes should have been fried a bit longer. I'm okay with that, I'll just leave a smaller tip."

Die stinky old man. Patricia thinks to herself.

With a look of concern, she then asks, "Would you like a new order?"

The man belches and sarcastically replies, "No, thanks, I can see how busy you are."

The waitress nods and smiles as she resumes to service the other tables.

The man then clutches the coffee cup, stands up and points to a television. "There's Stein. Quiet! Let's hear what the jailbird has to say."

Local Yokels

Silverware ceases to clash as all heads turn to the television. Conversations are brought down to a whisper. On the television screen is a news reporter wearing a blaze orange parka.

The red-faced woman says, "Hello, this is Vicky Markus for Channel Six News. Good morning and welcome back to our coverage of the tenth anniversary of the Unicorn Massacre." With snow swirling in front of her face, she continues. "Today, I'm standing where the ice is over nine inches thick, hoping to talk to the author of the book, 'Shoestring Strangler'."

The camera's view slowly expands to include a small shack out on the lake.

Pointing to the shack, the reporter then says, "Ever since Dean Stein was released from prison, that's where he spends most of his time."

The camera then focuses in on the shack that is built on large wooden skis.

"And today is a big day for Mr. Stein. Tonight, is the sold-out movie première based on his book."

Walking into the camera's frame is a large man wearing a brown and tan, camouflage snowsuit.

While the large man walks toward her, she says, "Let's see if Mr. Stein will answer some questions."

As the man trudges closer, his fox fur hat comes into view. With the snow whipping in his face, he walks by the news reporter.

Determined to get a reaction, Vicky blurts, "Mr. Stein do you know anything that can help investigators in capturing who is responsible for killing and dismembering eight of your neighbors, including your wife?"

Ignoring the question, the man adjusts his backpack. He then continues to walk to the shack. Trying to keep up with Dean the reporter loses her footing. But before she falls to the ground the burly man reaches out and snatches her up by the arm.

Again, trying to pry open his emotions, the persistent reporter says, "Some say your book is a compilation written from interviews you've had with the real killer. Is this true?"

Seeing that she has her footing back, the man lets go of her arm and continues to walk toward the shanty.

The reporter chases after him and pleads, shouting in the wind, "Mr. Stein do you know who the Shoestring Strangler is?"

With the man in the background headed for the shack, Vicky then states, "Well, it looks like Mr. Stein is sticking to his vow not to talk to reporters."

A gust of wind makes the rest of the reporter's words inaudible.

To block the wind, the reporter then turns her body, "It's a big day for Moon Lake too. Several events are scheduled. And we'll be broadcasting live updates from all of these events. So, stay tuned to Channel Six. For right now, this is Vicky Marcus for Channel Six News. Back to you Lou."

Inside the television studio, the camera focuses in on a newsman wearing a pressed black suit and burgundy tie.

"Thank you, Vicky."

Sitting behind the golden-oak desk, the anchorman ponders aloud.

"Will we ever know what really happened inside the theater on that horrific night? And, will the Shoestring Strangler ever be caught? Coming after these commercials, we'll talk to two professionals who assist law enforcement in capturing serial killers. Also, when we come back from a short commercial break, I will announce the winners of the chauffeured limousine ride to tonight's big movie première. Yes, someone's going to win two front-row tickets to the movie, Shoestring Strangler. Movie critics are hailing it an instant classic."

It's now or never

Judy sits at the mahogany vanity and brushes her long black hair. She looks at pictures and mementos that line the mirror. Her eyes finally come to rest on a picture of Janis and her. At the time of the picture they were just teenagers.

Looking at their silly pose, taken inside a photo-booth, she reminisces.

We did some really stupid things. Like when we put that crazy parrot in the principal's office. And, when the principle came on the intercom wanting to know who put the bird in his office. You could hear the bird cussing. We laughed so hard it hurt. Even our teacher laughed.

Hearing the phone ting, Judy picks it up to see that Lexis had sent her a text message.

It's like the universe has erupted into a feeding frenzy! Tyrannical vampires are running wild gorging themselves with innocent blood.

Judy dials Lexis's number. "Hi Lex, staying busy?"

"Last night, the diner was packed. I did not get off work until two in the morning. I barely got any sleep. It felt like some silly ghost was tickling my nose with a feather that smelled like soap."

Nodding her head, Judy replies, "I know what you mean. It's crazy. And with all this snow I decided that I'm not going to Dean's party. I know he was proven innocent, but he still creeps me out. Besides, I told Jen I'd help her at the lodge tonight."

"Yea, Randy has gone to a lot of trouble arranging the talent show. Did you know that Charlene will be there? She's a great singer. And she's known for introducing new talent to the world. And, that's why I'm on my way to the lodge to rehearse."

"You're going to the lodge?"

"Yea, after I pick up Sandy and her friend, Zongzi."

"Where are you picking them up?"

"I'm meeting them at the diner. I hope the roads are clear, it's really snowing."

Thinking of all the victims of the Shoestring Strangler, Judy eyes fills with tears.

Judy says depressingly, "I still can't get over what's happening."

Feeling her sadness, Lexis says, "I know what you mean, I have never seen anything like this. Moon Lake's like a pulsating black hole. Don't worry Jude we'll get through this together."

Judy replies. "Well, I've got to get ready. Going to the theater to set up tables and heat up food."

"Okay Judy, I'll see ya later."

Judy says goodbye and continues to brush her hair. Behind the clutter of perfume bottles, earring trees and lotion she pulls out a picture. It is a picture of her husband and her fishing off the lodge's pier. Looking deep into the picture, she smiles admiring the setting sun reflecting off the lake.

"That was one of the best days of my life. It was perfect." Changing her train of thought, she thinks about Lexis. *It's been her dream to be a ventriloquist. She's going to be great tonight. I really want to see her new act.*

Who done it?

Looking around the crowed diner, Sandy turns to Zongzi, "Clear your mind and think positive."

"Sandy, how did you become so superstitious?"

"Finish your pancakes and maybe I'll tell you."

Zongzi sighs and complies. He pours maple syrup over what is left of his pancakes and eats them.

He then says, "Okay Sandy, I am done eating so tell me why."

Hearing the bell above the diner's door jingle, Sandy looks up and says, "There's Lexis"

Zongzi turns to see a very attractive woman walking toward them.

Feeling his heart thump, he thinks. *She looks just like Patricia. They could pass as twins.*

Seeing Sandy and Zongzi, Lexis waves her hand. Wearing a light blue turtleneck sweater and embroidered jeans, she makes her way through the busy diner. Also wearing ear-buds and holding her phone, Lexis walks to their table.

Thinking out loud Zongzi says. "Now that's sex appeal. What a smile. I just want to swim in those eyes."

Sandy whispers to Zongzi. "Calm down and don't say anything that might freak her out."

Sitting down at the table with them, Lexis is seemingly unaffected by all the commotion in the diner.

Talking to her phone Lexis says. "Okay, you've already told me. I got to go, I am here so I we'll talk later. Frustrated, Lexis rolls her eyes and takes out her ear-buds.

She looks at Sandy, "So, how's my Physic Counselor?"

"I'm doing good. This is Zongzi?"

Lexis turns to Zongzi, "Hello Zong, nice to meet you." Looking back at Sandy, Lexis continues to say, "It was just like this last night. This place was jammed packed. When I punched out, people were still coming in." Lexis hands a small box to Sandy. "Oh yea, here's a present for you."

While Sandy peels off the wrapping paper Zongzi thinks to himself. *That voice! Oh, so sexy.*

Sandy then says, "I hope it's some of that perfume you're wearing." Opening the box Sandy sees the small perfume bottle and smiles. "Thanks Lex."

"Your welcome cuz. So, can you see it? The over packed spiritual baggage that has turned this place into a cesspool? I can feel it twist in my gut. Like when I saw those big-eyed aliens. Yea, all this poop is stirring up a lot of bad memories." Sandy replies. "Lex, let's keep our eyes looking forward. But you're right this place is getting to me too. If you already had breakfast can you give us a ride to the lodge?"

"It's crazy their too, they're getting ready to hold a talent contest." Zongzi interjects.

Looking around the diner, witnessing the festive like atmosphere, Sandy sighs in disbelief and says, "What is with this town? Isn't anyone worried about the Shoestring Strangler?"

Zongzi says, "I agree with what the lodge's bartender said last night. You might as well take advantage of all people in town and make some money."

Walking out of the kitchen door, a man wearing a cook's hat walks up to Lexis.

"Lexis, can you call in another order? We're running out of everything."

She nods her head, takes out her phone and puts in her ear-buds.

"I'll do it right now."

Sitting at a nearby table, wanting to hear the newscast, a man sets down a coffee cup and stands.

Pointing to the television he shouts, "Hey! Can you tone it down please? I want to hear the TV?"

The people eating inside the diner comply and bring their conversations down to a whisper.

From the television a baritone voice is heard.

"This is Lou Trudeau for Channel Six. Here today, on this tenth-year anniversary of the Unicorn Massacre is Psychiatrist Dr. Mary Ulrich, and Psychologist Dr. Henry Strumpell." The newscaster clears his throat and continues, "Dr. Strumpell and Dr. Ulrich are criminal profilers. Dr. Strumpell what is a profiler?"

A confident gentleman's voice replies, "Certainly. We help apprehend serial killers by being a magnifying glass into their psyche. We assist investigators in anticipating the extraordinary troubled individual's next move. We use logical or illogical patters to predict the subject or subject's next move."

Reading from his notes, the newsman says, "And now to bring into the mix, is Dr. Mary Ulrich. Being a psychiatrist, can you give us your two cents worth?"

A female voice with a soft Indian accent quickly injects, "Mr. Trudeau that is the brainiest economic value that you could request from me. We all contain two inner senses. One loving and the other is the direct opposite. Provided it complements the other, our psyche's independence is validated because it provides equilibrium. In a healthy environment these senses can help us to endure life's physical and mental challenges. In the case of the Unicorn Massacre, the perpetrator is combating a deep-rooted distressing event. With no compunction to face the reality of this traumatic incident, induces falsehoods. From that point on all mental processes are rerouted. The killer's turmoil removes love as the internal guiding light. This faux interpretation of internal and external stimulus, results in a disconnection to the purpose of life. Fueled by ego or greed, these misconceptions suffocate logical thoughts. And in an attempt to counterbalance, the mind invokes sensory images and self-constructed illusions to sow relief. However, with this intense induction these distorted visualizations inhibit normal mental processes. It's logical to assume that whoever is responsible for the strangulations and dismemberment is suffering from uncontrollable internal and external mental hostilities. So, in conjunction with the autopsy, the Unicorn Massacre was due to complex homicidal violence. This conclusion is non-speculative and empirical."

The newsman then says, "To gain perspective, I know that you both keep a scientific disconnection to the facts of the crime. However, I lost count of how many four syllable words you used. So, Dr. Ulrich can you break it down into simpler terms?"

The astute psychiatrist then rephrases her insight, "The Shoestring Strangler, in order to lead a purposeful life, has instituted a self-imposed reality. The idiosyncrasies are invoked instantaneously when the individual is looking for a painless way out of an unsettling moment. To cope with life, the synapses in the brain misfire."

Lou turns to his other guest, "Dr. Strumpell being a world-renowned psychologist, what's your insight into the mindset of the killer? And if a killer is found to have a mental defect, should they be held responsible for their crimes?"

The reserved psychologist calmly strokes his beard. "Analyzing the trail left behind, the subject's brain activity is fueled by an irresistible passion of self-expression. Their selfish impulses cloud healthy thought processes. Perverse, self-serving thoughts fester and snowball until the subject loses touch with reality. From within the pith of the psychical process, trying to find solace, the mind surrenders to irrepressible compulsions. When fully aroused their irrational thoughts are then self-rationalized. This deranged mind is submersed into their perverse fantasies. This self-affliction relentlessly picks at their will and eventually they become mindless. Like a zombie, they carry out the deed. In basic terms, the crux of the affliction is their self-perceived inadequacies that contaminate normal thought processes. In conclusion the Shoestring Strangler, in order to survive, finds self-importance by having control and complete mastery of their victims. Answering your second question, even though mentally disturbed people know the difference between right and wrong, it's up to the judge. The judge considers mental evaluations and makes his decision. In this case, I agree with Dr. Ulrich that this intense fervor behind these acts insinuates that this individual cannot stop themselves. The bloody overkill, the flaunting note and the moniker, all reveal a deeper psychosis driven by a narcissistic ego."

Baffled by information overload, the newsman inquires, "So, Dr. Strumpell, can you please explain to us, the ones who don't understand psychobabble. How do profilers help authorities to catch killers?"

Dr. Strumpell replies. "Knowing the neurosis of the killers will outline behavior patterns. Using these patterns will assist authorities on who the killer is and what the killer's next move could be."

"And, in conjunction with studies based on case files of past serial killers, we believe the killer or killers will strike again." Dr. Ulrich interjects.

Needing to wrap up the interview, the newsman says, "I want to thank both of you for your insights."

"Mr. Trudeau, May I give some advice?" Dr. Strumpell inquires courteously,

"Make it fast." the newsman says urgently.

Speaking slowly and clearly the Psychologist says, "The killer's biological defense mechanisms have been skewed. For them to work properly and procure positive mental processes, the Shoestring Strangler must find tranquility from within. And that holds true for anyone. At the end of the day, relieve yourself from anxiety and stress. The process is simple. Position your mind and body to relax. Then, breathe deep and sleep well."

The newsman rushing to a close quickly says. "Thank you Dr. Strumpell and Dr. Ulrich. Later tonight, we'll hear another perspective. Vicky Marcus interviews Moon Lake's very own Sherlock Homes, Private Detective, Robert Sentieri. He was the original detective assigned to investigate the Unicorn slayings. And, in closing this morning's broadcast, here's a video tribute for the victims who lives were taken from them ten years ago today. For Channel Six Morning News, this is Lou Trudeau. Enjoy your day."

While a soothing violin solo plays in the back ground, a video shows the news line of the murderous trail left by the Shoestring Strangler. From the Unicorn massacre through Dean's prison release. The pictures and headlines bring the viewers up to date. Faces in the diner lose expression and their eyes glaze over filling with deep sadness. The video tribute shows pictures of the victims with vibrant smiles. Seemingly frozen in time, their lives flash by on the television screen. A woman lets out a mournful cry. The dishwasher and the cook walk out of the kitchen to see what the commotion is all about.

The stocky cook points to the television and says, "There's a picture of my cousins, Jose and Emanuel."

The picture is of two boys playing their guitars around a campfire.

The cook adds, "You know that Jose is the one who taught me how to play the banjo. Look, there's Jason and John having a food fight at the diner. They were always goofing around."

"I was there when that happened, and I got hit in the face with vanilla ice-cream. Wow, it feels like yesterday." the dishwasher interjects.

Again, pointing at the television the cook says. "That's Jason in his high school letter jacket. I didn't know he had all those track ribbons."

Another picture shows Janis hugging a droopy eared puppy. That picture fades to a photo of Julie and Shannon flexing their muscles on a tennis court. That photo fades into the two young friends walking along a ridge that overlooks Moon Lake. As the video ends, a list of credits scrolls across the television screen.

A caption then comes into focus. "The violin music used for this tribute was recorded live ten years ago at the Moon Lake Christmas recital. It was Shannon's last performance."

The closing picture is close up of Shannon's face, playing her violin with her tongue sticking out.

Following the video, a commercial comes on about plastic surgery as the crowd noise fills the diner. A man then walks up and turns the television off.

Sounding irritated, the man bellows. "Sherlock Homes? Sentieri doesn't' know squat."

Soon after his comment, the buzz inside the diner grows into a frenzy while patrons theorize who they think the killer is.

A man putting on his winter coat and gloves speaks out, "It's always someone you'd never suspect."

Sitting at the counter a gray bearded man wearing a baseball hat says, "The Shoestring Strangler is a government agent sent here to create chaos."

Mystified, Zongzi turns to Lexis, "Beautiful woman I have never smelled such a tantalizing perfume. Maybe that's why everyone losing their minds?"

Staring off in the distance, seemingly in deep thought, she does not answer.

Trying to snap her out of it, Sandy says discreetly. "I've talked to Detective Sentieri. He said that he believes that the DNA that was recovered at the Chicago crime scene will prove Dean's innocence." Seeing that she has her attention, Sandy continues. "And, while talking to him, he reassured me that Dean was not the killer. But he did say it's probably someone who lives in Moon Lake. He also said that they have decoded the note found at the Chicago scene. It said that, 'On the tenth anniversary, when the clock strikes eight, two more shoestrings will be tied'." Seeing the pain in Lexis's gaze, Sandy adds, "Lexis, Zongzi and I are going to do our best to stop this madness."

"Yes, we're here to do exactly that." Zongzi says reassuringly. Feeling as if someone is breathing down her neck, Sandy says. "Can we go to the lodge to talk?"

"Well, I hope you guys aren't disappointed in me." Lexis replies bashfully. "You see, I'm on my way there to rehearse with Candio. I've entered us in the talent contest. The contest starts at nine o'clock tonight, so I really want to go over my material."

Sounding relieved, Zongzi says, "That's right you're a ventriloquist. The owner of the lodge, Randy, told me that you're the favorite to win." He turns to Sandy and adds. "So, what do you say? How about you and me enter the contest?" With an excited tone of voice Lexis says. "For the best performance they're giving a luxury cruise, for two, around the world!"

Still looking at Sandy, Zongzi pleads. "Come on. You sing, play guitar and I'll play harmonica."

Missing persons

On the first floor of the Moon Lake Police department a police officer studies a bulletin board.

Looking at a collection of faces, descriptions and dates of last seen, she thinks; *Missing person reports are up twenty percent since last year. Where are all these people?*

Slowly subdued by her beige office cubical and cluttered desktop, she turns to gaze at a computer screen. She is mesmerized watching the screensaver rotate through photographs of her week in Jamaica. Pictures of sandcastles, beachfronts and sunsets fade in and out. Daydreaming, she feels the tropical breeze blow against her skin. Listening to the waves roll in, she smiles and sighs. Pulling her back to her duties the telephone rings.

She answers, "Hello, Moon Lake Police Department, can I help you."

On the phone, a woman with a Spanish accent replies, "My daughter and her husband are not home from work." With a child crying in the background her voice shakes as she says, "They should be home by now. I don't know what to do."

"Calm down. Please tell me their names?"

Desperately, the caller complies. "Martha and Gildardo."

With the realization of a serial killer on the loose, the police officer sidesteps the directive of waiting twenty-four hours to initiate action. She spins around in her chair and begins to fill out the missing person report. From the onset of the phone call, she has had a sick feeling in her gut.

With the form completed and before hanging up the phone, she says calmly, "A police officer will be right over and if there is any news, I will call you right away."

After hanging up the phone the woman taps her pen on the desktop. Following her intuition, she makes a phone call.

A man's voice answers the phone. "Hello, this is Moon Lake's Homicide Division. Can I help you?"

"This is Ann in Missing Persons can you please have Agent Mahoney call me?"

"Hold on, he's in a meeting."

As blood races through her veins the police officer waits on hold.

In less than a minute she hears a deep voice, "Yea, this is Agent Mahoney, go ahead."

"I just received a missing person's report."

The man listens while she fills him in on the specifics of the report. When she is finished, he thinks to himself; *That's the young couple who lives in the targeted neighborhood.*

Agent Mahoney ten replies, "Thanks for reporting this to me. It's good to see that you trusted your gut. Sometimes it's all we got to go on. And until further notice all reports are to be immediately funneled to me."

"Yes sir."

"Don't call me sir. My name is Jack."

Agent Mahoney then presses a button on the phone and says in an authoritative tone, "Get over to Gildardo and Martha's house"

A voice on the phone replies. "Yes. I know them personally. They should be just getting home from the meat packing plant."

"They are missing so try to get a recent photo of them both. And get Sentieri on the phone ASAP."

Agent Mahoney puts the phone down, opens a vanilla folder and shuffles through a stack of papers.

"Here it is the potential victims list. Looks like the profilers were right. All the victims live in the same neighborhood."

Who's your worst nightmare

Miles south of Moon Lake, camped alongside a busy street, a homeless woman rubs her eyes. A man walks by and she reaches out to the stranger. The man reaches down and hands her a dollar bill. She smiles and thanks the man. However, the pain does not drain from her mind.

Talking to herself she says, "Thank you for I have nothing, nobody and nowhere to go."

The woman straightens out her back and snowflakes slide off her soiled pink snowsuit. She takes out a lighter, picks up a cigarette-butt and then lights it. She leans back and takes a slow draw. Looking up at the towering red brick building she lets out a puff of smoke. Looking up at the skyline she watches the smoke drifts upward.

On the fourteenth floor a tiger striped kitten slowly lurks across the floor stalking a mouse. The kitten freezes in place. Quickly leaping it pounces, bites onto the mouse and scurries away with it underneath a bed.

Nearby, on a bedside table a telephone vibrates. Startling the kitten, it zips into another room. Underneath the brown tobacco stained ceiling, stretched out on a bed is a graying dark-haired man.

Mumbling, he whispers, "No."

Restless, the man rolls over slipping into a deep slumber. Inside a dream he is gagged with his arms tied up around a streetlight pole. Frustrated, he watches as a dark shadow sneaks up on an unsuspecting young boy. He tries desperately to break free as the fiend puts a garrote around the boy's neck. Tightening the garrote, the boy opens his mouth as he is lifted off the ground. The boy's face turns red as he kicks his feet. Still trying to break free he sees tears form and roll down the child's face. Losing consciousness, the boy stares into the eyes of the smiling strangler.

Helplessly still tied to the pole he hears the killer whisper, "Who's your worst nightmare?"

The dreamer's voice fills with anger. "Where are you? Where did you go?"

From out of the darkness of his mind he then hears a boisterous laugh.

A blurry figure comes out of the shadows.

"No one can stop me."

The dreamer replies. "You're not going to get away this time?"

Hearing a loud rumble, the man wakes up. He then rolls over to see a telephone vibrating on the table.

Sitting up he stretches out. Wearing a tee-shirt and boxer shorts the man sits on the edge of the bed. The sleepy man then again eyes the phone. He picks it up to hear a computerized voice.

"Good morning. This is you seven-thirty AM wake up call."

After hanging up the telephone, with a raspy voice, he says. "Good morning?"

Yawning, he looks over at a photograph lying on the table. "There we are. My beautiful daughter and my ex-wife. We were happy at one time. This picture had to be taken before the killings. Lori is still in braces. Dam, that roller-coaster scared the shit out of me."

The man turns the photo over and reads the scribbled message on the back. "Happy birthday asshole!"

Wiping the sleep from his eyes, he thinks; *Me and the Ex had our moments.* The man sighs. *My heart aches not knowing where my daughter is. I can't believe that Lori's thirty already. I haven't heard from her since she walked out of the treatment center two years ago. Why won't she call me.*

Yawning he reaches over and grabs a tobacco bag. After rolling a cigarette, he becomes frustrated trying to light it. He tosses the butane lighter onto the ground and grabs some matches. When the cigarette is lit, he takes a puff. Looking down the twisted cigarette he watches it burn. The stress relieving tobacco flavor soothes him. He takes the cigarette out of his mouth and taps it over the ashtray that is on the bedside table. Exhaling, he gazes through the white curling tobacco smoke. The man then looks around the room.

"This is the filthiest hotel I have ever been in. Oh well, it's the cheapest too."

Feeling the day ahead begin to close in on him, he thinks; *I knew Dean was innocent. Lexis told me that Janis and he argued, but I don't think he'd kill her. And, what they did to Dean during the interrogation, anyone would have confessed.* The man continues to ponders; *But, how did Dean know who the killer killed first, second and so on. No one knew that until the ME told us days after his confession. Something fishy?* The kitten leaps up, scratches its way up the man's leg and curls in his lap. The man pets the kitten. After enjoying another puff, again he taps the cigarette over the ashtray. He then puts the kitten down onto the floor.

Standing, he grabs the newspaper and makes his way into the kitchen. He fills the coffeepot up with water and walks over to a small round table. The wood chair creaks as he sits down. He then begins to read the newspaper; *Shoestring Strangler promises to strike at eight o'clock tonight.*

While the coffeemaker peculates, his mind reads between the lines. *There's too much going on here for one person to be responsible. The deed is too calculated and precise.*

Reading further about the killer he reaffirms an apparent fact; "They were too comfortable within the Chicago crime scene and that made them sloppy."

He reads on till the coffeepot stops peculating. Putting the paper down he walks over and fills up a cup coffee. When he sits back down at the table, the kitten rubs against his leg. Reaching down, he picks up the kitten and places it on the table.

Scratching the kitten behind the ears he says, "Bonkers, the path to the truth starts with Dean. After interrogators finally made him snap, he had an odd reaction. He jokingly said that on the night of the killings he had turned into a wolf. He then correctly demonstrated how the killer made the shoestring into a garrote. Included in his false confession, he stated the correct order in which the victims were killed. This order was later proven by the forensic evidence."

Contemplating, his mind drifts into the past.

We attended the same high school. Back then, before they got married, Janis and Dean performed in a band together. We didn't hang around the same crowd. But growing up in a small town our paths often crossed.

He remembers back to when Dean was young. How he delivered newspapers and did yard work for the Fitzgerald's, the elderly couple who had no children.

"Since he's release from prison Aunt Mary's said that he came over to visit and repaired the steps leading up her front porch. Yea, everyone likes him. He is kind of a loner. And how did he know the gory details of the killings?" The man takes another sip of coffee. "Don't over think it. Stick to the facts." The man lets out a sigh and then puts down the cup of coffee. "Okay, let's try this again."

Determined, he envisions the surreal moment of seeing the ghastly scene inside the Unicorn Theater.

"The carnage was sickening. Walking into that theater and seeing all that blood splattered on the theater's screen, I asked myself. What kind of person could do this?" "The facts are that, Dean Stein, the theater's janitor was found unconscious behind the concession stand. For reasons unknown, he was the only suspect ever investigated. Now that DNA evidence has cleared him. Since his release Dean has already regained the respect of most of the residents of Moon Lake."

As he sits there and contemplates, a couple more factual barbs come to mind.

"Not only is he a decorated war veteran and a successful taxidermist, Dean has a heart of gold."

Reminiscing, he shakes his head displeasingly.

He's the last person, I thought, I 'd ever have to put handcuffs on. Man, that was tuff. But I had to do it. It's my job. Later on, after Dean had waived his right to have an attorney present during the interrogation, he was shoved into the interview room. That's when investigators began to beat on him. They slammed him around until he screamed for mercy. Everyone seemed to overlook this abuse because of the severity of the crime. When he finally broke down, Dean admitted to the killings and signed a confession. The confession included why and how he killed them.

"But what I can't figure out is that Dean did not struggle for the words. Also, he convincingly demonstrated how he dismembered the bodies with his hunting knife. And every time he told the story, he became more dramatic in his descriptions. He also joked that he didn't shed a tear when he chopped off Janis's arms and legs. He scoffed describing how he had tossed her body pieces off the stage. When investigators ask why he propped the bodies in the front row of the theater. Dean calmly stated that he was lonely and didn't want to watch the movie alone."

Staring off into space the man hears his stomach growl. He puts several pieces of pizza on a plate and puts the plate into the microwave.

While warming the pizza, he pours himself another cup of coffee and continues to think over puzzling facts.

During the interrogation Dean said that all he wanted was to go down in history as the bloodiest killer of all time. When he made that statement everyone in that interrogation room was convinced that they had their killer. And when the preliminary forensics report came back it confirmed most of Dean's story. Except that the report included pictorial evidence proving that the bodies were dismembered using a serrated edge and not by Dean's hunting knife.

Taking a sip off the hot coffee the groggy man ponders aloud. "You'd think everyone else saw what the facts proved, but they didn't. They'd already convinced themselves that Dean was the killer. They couldn't see that he was saying only what they wanted to hear. I knew Dean loved Janis and there's no way that he'd kill her. When I visited him in jail, he told me that without her there was nothing else to live for. He did not like jail, but he did say that it saved his life. I'm glad that I visited him in prison. I really got to know the man."

Finished drinking the coffee, he fills the cup up again and puts the newspaper under his arm. Walking into the bathroom, he sits down on the toilet. After placing his coffee cup down on the rim of the bathtub, he begins to read the newspaper. With his mind racing the words become blurred and he loses concentration

He puts the paper down and thinks back to Dean's trial.

He sat stoic throughout, showing no emotion. Until he heard that he could receive the death penalty. That's when Dean agreed to plead guilty in exchange for a life sentence. Then, when the judge's gavel fell, I wasn't the only one in that courtroom who was disappointed. Most of the family's members of the victims also believed that Dean had nothing to do with the killings. We all knew that the real killer was still out there.

The man then gets up off the toilet and flushes it.

After washing his hands in the sink, he wipes shaving cream on his face.

"That's why when he was in prison Dean wrote that book. He knew that a convicted killer can't profit from a crime." He then begins to shave and taps the razor against the sink. "He wanted to help out the best way he could."

Searching for more facts, he remembers being called in by the FBI to go over the Chicago crime scene.

Walking into that bloody alleyway, I had the same feeling I did when I walked into the theater. I knew that the Shoestring Strangler had resurfaced. When investigating the bloody scene, the method of operation confirmed my gut feeling. I won't be surprise when the DNA evidence recovered at the Chicago crime scene is a match to the DNA evidence collected inside the theater.

Using the razor, he swipes the remaining lather off his face. He then turns off the water and splashes on aftershave lotion on his face. Feeling the alcohol bite into his skin, he looks over his face.

Dam, I'm getting old. So, what's the motive? At both crime scenes all the victims' valuables remained intact, so robbery is out the question. None of the victims' bodies were abused, suggest that the crimes were not sexually motivated. However, because of the horrific dismemberment and signs cabalism, the motivation was deep and personal. And there's one fact that stands out. How the victims' bodies were positioned. The limbless torsos propped up in the seats of the theater. And at the Chicago murder scene the boy was propped up using the street pole. All victims were left with a neatly tied shoestring around their neck.

The detective slowly moves his head side to side in disgust. *The killer most likely lives in Moon Lake and definitely knew the victims. Profilers did agree that the killer's suffering from a psychotic disorder. However, the very involved and personal manner in which the carnage was carried out, whoever it is, is highly motivated.*

After securing his dental work, the man looks into the mirror and adjusts the collar on his shirt. He puts on a maroon colored tie with silver pin stripes.

Adjusting the tie, he says. "I better hurry up. Got to be out that door by quarter after eight. Or I'll miss the remembrance ceremony."

Precious moments

Sitting on a neatly made bed looking through a photo album, Lloyd wipes tears from his eyes.

"God, thanks for blessing us with Shannon. I remember when Ida first asked me about adopting a child. I thought that if You wanted us to have a child, we would of have had one of our own. I know different now. When Shannon reached out to me with those little hands, my heart filled with love."

From outside the room Lloyd hears his wife's voice.

"Are you in Shannon's room?"

Washing the dishes, scrubbing a pan, Ida thinks; *I pray that today is the day we can get some closure. I think of Shannon every day. I remember when we took our little girl to the zoo. She got so excited watching the monkeys. And how can I forget when she first learned how to ride a two-wheel bike. She was so proud. I can still hear her little voice. 'Look at me!' Like her first day of school, when she told us, 'Don't worry, school's not a bad place.' Shannon was such a caring soul. She was our shining light.* Rinsing off her hands she dries them off with a towel.

"God please carry us through this day."

Ida puts the towel down and walks through the quiet home. She goes into the room where her husband is.

"Lloyd we've been partners in life for forty years and you've never went back on your word. So, are we going to clean out this room?"

The teary-eyed elderly man looks up for a moment before he continues to look at photos.

"Remember this picture? It was when Shannon was blowing out the candles on her tenth birthday?"

"Yes, she and I baked her cake." Ida sits down beside him and then says, "Come on, we have to get ready to go to the theater. Everything is already set up. There's going to be a lot of people there and I just hope that I made enough meatballs." Her husband says. "Sweetheart, I wish I could go back in time and give that little girl just one more hug. We were so happy. Those were the best days of my life."

Ida looks around the room. Seeing Shannon's pictures and awards, flood her mind with memories.

"Lloyd, it's time to clean out this room. We can give all this stuff to Saint Vincent DePaul thrift store."

As if he didn't hear his wife Lloyd says, "She was so talented."

Ida replies. "She was a God sent."

Lloyd nods his head in agreement.

"Okay Ida, I'll take down the bed, box up everything and get rid of it. Except for her violin, we're keeping that."

"Okay dear. But don't forget that we were blessed with raising Lexis while Dean was in prison."

"Yea, Lexis was a hand full. My blood pressure went down the day she moved out to live with her sister."

"Lloyd, Lexis wants us to go to the lodge tonight to see her new act."

Sinister gaze

In pitch-black darkness, Martha slowly regains consciousness and finds her mouth taped shut. Sensing that her wrists and ankles are tightly taped also, her eyes widen.

Groggy, she thinks to herself; *Oh no, Gildardo, where are you?*

She sits up and moving her lips she begins to loosen the tape on her mouth. She continues to stretch out her mouth and then constrict her lips. Feeling the grip of the adhesive separate from her skin, she uses her shoulder to eventually swipe the gummy tape from off her mouth.

Using her teeth, she then gnaws and rips the tape off her wrist. After tearing off the tape around her ankles she stands up and feels around the room. Realizing that she is a prisoner of the Shoestring Strangler, her heart thumps in her chest and she begins to sob. She tries to calm her thoughts as she continues to feel around in the dark. Her fingers come across a door. Franticly she twists the door handle back and forth to see if she can open it. Knowing that she is trapped, she prays.

God, please help me to be strong. To find a way back home to my family.

The fear of being helplessly alone twists in her gut.

What happened in that alley?

Surrendering to emotions, Martha sits down and moans distressingly.

God please take care of grandma and our daughter. Grandma may not see well but she has a sharp mind.

Realizing that worrying about things she cannot control does not help her situation. She breaths deep trying to calm herself.

"If I want to survive, I going to have to calm myself down."

With her family in her thoughts, she continues to pray.

Most merciful God, thank You for Your blessings. Your graces fulfill us and Your gifts of love lighten our burdens. In our hour of darkness, You are the light that guides us to everlasting love. Please give us the strength to carry out Your glorious plan. And I beg You to please help us.

Hearing keys clink makes her heart jump. She then hears a key turn in the door lock. Martha hunches along the wall and hides her face. Hearing the door open, she listens closely. As footsteps approach, her bones ache in fear. When the footsteps cease, Martha can hear someone breathe and her muscles tighten. Terror stricken, she holds her breath. Trying to block out reality, Martha calmly tries to fill her mind with loving memories. She envisions one of the happiest moments of her life. Holding her daughter for the first time. Seeing Gildardo gleaming with pride. Hearing the footsteps turn and walk away, Martha takes in a relieving breath of air. Spellbound by the fading footsteps, Martha feels faint. Hearing the door slam shut, she tries to get to her feet. However, feeling woozy, she plops back down. Sitting there she tries to suppress the sick feeling in her stomach. Leaning against the wall she rubs her eyes. She then follows the wall back to the doorway and discovers a paper bag. Martha then senses a sinister gaze upon her. She feels her hair stand on end. Filled with dread, she is afraid to look, but she does anyways. Looking up she sees someone looking at her through a small window on the door. Making eye contact, her spine twitches. Thinking about her husband, she clasps her hands over her ears and begins to sob.

The promise

With sparrows chasing it, a red tail hawk flaps it's wings against the gray snowy sky. Flying over the snow-covered lake, smoke rises from a fishing shanty. The wooden structure creaks fighting off the winter winds.

Sitting inside on a short wooden stool, a stout man adjusts his fox fur hat. He drops a fishing line into a circular hole cut into the thick ice. The scruffy brown-haired man relaxes his mind watching the fishing line.

He jiggles the line and whispers, "I have all day."

Hearing his stomach moan, he sets the fishing pole on the ground. To prevent it from being yanked into the fishing hole, he sets his foot on the handle of the fishing pole.

Stroking his graying beard, he thinks; *Time for a break.*

He pulls off his deerskin mittens and rubs his weathered hands over a small propane heater. Leaning back, he stretches out his arms before he reaches for a black metal thermos. He then unscrews the plastic lid that doubles as a cup and fills it. He cautiously sips the steamy liquid.

"Ida's chicken soup, always hit's the spot."

He puts the cup down and tunes in small transistor radio. Coming out the fuzzy static, a man's exaggerated voice says, "I'm not a mountain climber, ski diver or tornado chaser. So, why would I be hanging around Moon Lake? Well, I'm not. I'm not a thrill seeker. I am miles away from the place and I'm not going there anytime soon. If I was mayor of Moon Lake, I'd cancel all events. And, I'd make sure that everyone stayed home with their windows and doors locked tight. And what about Dean Stein, did you read his book? Are you going to the movie tonight? Do you think that it is a perverse way of reopening wounds and re-victimizing the families? What do you think?"

Talking to himself Dean says. "Tell me what you think, shit for brains."

Almost as if he is daring a response, Dean glares at the radio. The voice again spews from the radio.

"Does the movie, with all the overpaid actors, glamorize one of the most pernicious killers of all time? I for one can't wait to see if the movie exposes the truth. Who knows, maybe a new perspective on the big screen will answer the big question. Who is the Shoestring Strangler? We can only hope. So, tell me what you think. Call or text me. All lines are open."

While Dean attentively continues to eye the fishing pole, he turns off the radio and says to himself, "I 'm just glad to have my life back. Being a fixture inside prison, day after day, almost drove me to take the easy way out. After I finally accepted the fact that God had me there for a reason, my anger just disappeared. I prayed every day for God to give me my life back. And now, here I am. I remember when the judge looked me in the eye and said, Mr. Stein, you're cleared from all charges. You're free. And you may leave through any door you wish."

Dean picks up the cup and takes another sip while his mind is immersed in memories of the past.

However, before his mind can sink deeper, he hears a bark outside the door. He places the cup of soup down, stands up and pushes the shanty's spring hinged door open.

Looking out the door, Dean says, "Hey, Tobias, where have you been?"

A black and tan, large pawed German Shepard prances inside, shakes the snow off and sniffs around the floor of the shanty. The dog then sticks his snoot into the bait bucket, watches the minnows swimming around and looks at the man. Dean says, "Toby, thanks for visiting me. I could use a buddy." The animal looks at him and tilts his head.

"I wonder if things will be any different after tonight. I can only hope."

The dog barks and wags his tail in response. Dean reaches into his pocket and pitches a piece of jerky into the air. Instantaneously the dog snatches the spicy treat in midair. The thick-furred animal then sniffs out a spot and gingerly lies down. Contently, while holding the chunk of jerky with his paws, the dog begins to gnaw on it.

Dean checks the fishing line.

"Tobias, I bet you like your meat rare? Don't you? Well if you ever get a chance to bite that asshole, Uncle Ted, bite him hard. And, I'll make sure you get all the rare meat you can eat. He has taken advantage of this tragedy to fatten the cities bank account." Dean leans over to fill up another cup of hot soup. "And, stop by the house tonight and I'll fill your belly." He takes a sip off the soup and scratches the dog on the head. "Toby, did you know that when I was in jail Ida visited me and put money in my commissary? I sure hope the movie doesn't disappoint her. I tried to get the director to see the story my way. The director said the way I wrote it was boring." Dean's face buckles trying to hold back an overflow of pent-up misery. "Maybe jail still is the safest place for me."

He thinks tenderly; *Janis, I can't count how many times in a day I see or hear something that reminds me of you. Remember our talks? How if one of us died that the other should find someone else. Well, tonight, I got a date with a very attractive woman. And, I still can't stop thinking about you.*

Dean chokes up.

"I will never get over you."

Stroking his beard Dean's mind reminisces romantic moments of the past. He then wipes away his tears, sips the hot broth and looks at the dog.

"My only buddy. You know it all still seems like a bad dream. I can't believe it has been ten years. But even though it happened so long ago, it seems like yesterday."

Outside the shanty the wind whips up and the shanty creaks. Dean sighs and whispers. "Yep Janis you were my everything."

Wink of an eye

Driving her car down the snowy street, Lexis turns on the windshield defroster.

Sitting alongside her in the front seat, Sandy looks to Lexis and says, "What's it like driving? Streets slippery?"

"In these conditions you have leave yourself plenty of room to stop. Just take it slow and you'll get there soon enough." Lexis looks into the rearview mirror and sees that Zongzi is staring at her ventriloquist doll. "Zong relax. I'll get you to the lodge in one piece. Besides, Candio already ate today."

Looking at Lexis's eyes in the review mirror, Zongzi replies, "Lexis, she's almost as pretty as you." He reaches over and strokes the dolls hair, "Candio, Lexis exhilarates me. Do you think her and I have a chance for romance?"

Hearing this, Sandy laughs and says. "Zongzi, you get exhilarated when the wind blows."

Shifting gears, Lexis says. "Zong, when we get to the lodge, can you carry Candio inside?"

"Yes, I can do that. But I rather carry you over the threshold. But we'd have to get married first."

"If you marry me, you marry Candio too."

Looking out of the corner of his eye Zongzi winks at the doll. "I hope you don't snore."

Lexis sees him wink and smiles.

"Zongzi, her heart is made of sulfur and her touch is cold as ice."

The car gets quiet while Zongzi thinks; *Lexis is so pretty, so sexy and crazy. Just my type.*

Sandy then says. "So, Detective Sentieri told me that Dean had nothing to do with your mother's death? Do you still think Dean had something to do with it?"

While she maneuvers through a busy intersection Lexis says, "I visited him in prison."

Lexis shifts gears and turns on the radio. The song, "Holly Jolly Christmas" plays while the wiper-blades brush aside snowflakes.

Interrupting the classic carol, the voice of a female is heard on the radio.

"The Shoestring Strangler has struck again. This morning in Moon Lake, a bloody scene was discovered in an alleyway located near the Unicorn Theater. The lead investigator report concurs; 'The crime scene is consistent with previous Shoestring Strangler murders.' A briefing from Police Headquarters has been scheduled." The news-reporter's voice continues spurting bloody descriptions of the alleyway. The car is quiet as a flurry of words streak across the airwaves. "At the crime scene, dismemberment and cannibalism was knotted together in a grotesque display of horror. The killer also left behind the infamous macabre memento. A shoestring tied neatly in a bow around the neck of the limbless victim's torso. Crime scene technicians also have discovered a coded note. And like the previous notes, it ended with the flauntingly flared signature; 'yours truly, Shoestring Strangler'."

Throw another log in the fire

Along the lakeshore eyes peer out through an ice frosted second story window. Watching a bushy black haired, bearded man, the light brown-haired woman smiles. Wearing a black snowsuit, the man carries firewood through the deep snow. The woman wearing black slacks and a red sweater walks down downstairs. Reaching the bottom of the stairs she flips a switch. Light reveals a dining and stage area. She walks into an adjoining room. She flips another switch that reveals a smaller dinning and bar area.

Coming in through the backdoor, carrying firewood the brown-eyed man looks at the woman and says, "Is the coffee ready?"

"I haven't even put it on yet."

Having taken off the snowsuit the man walks into the room wearing blue-jean pants and a blue and black checkered flannel shirt. Carrying split wood logs, he walks to a stone-faced fireplace and stacks logs. The woman spoons coffee grounds into the coffee maker and pours water into it. After she turns it on, she hit's a button on the cash register. The cash register beeps and begins to spit out a receipt.

Seeing the man lighting a fire in the fireplace, she looks at a picture on the wall. It is a picture of her and the man sitting on the pier with the sun setting over the lake.

The woman thinks to herself; *He's been so stressed. I wonder what he will say when I tell him about the pregnancy test.*

With the fireplace lit the man walks to the front door. After unlocking the door, he walks back toward the woman who is behind the bar. The woman comes out from behind the bar to meet him. They kiss, and she begins to roll up his sleeves of his shirt.

Looking tenderly into his eyes, she says, "You think that's that enough firewood?"

"It'll last through the afternoon."

The woman sits down on a bar stool and using a knife she begins to slice up a lemon. The man turns on the television and sits down next to her.

Changing channels, he says, "Did you hear about what happened?"

"Yea, they discovered a slain body in an alleyway."

The man sighs in disbelief.

The woman responds saying, "Randy, do you think we should call off the talent show?"

"I think the show will be a well needed distraction."

The woman quickly adds, "That reminds me. I have to take out more fish. A party of seven is coming in for lunch."

The front door swings open and Sandy, Lexis and Zongzi rush in from the cold. In the foyer, Zongzi places Lexis's doll on the ground. Sandy and Lexis also put boxes down. After taking off their heavy winter coats the three of them join the couple at the bar.

Shaking off the chill, Lexis says, "That coffee sure smells good. Randy, I sure am glad you have the fireplace lit already. It's freezing out there."

Behind the bar, wiping out ashtrays, the woman turns the television down and says, "If it isn't the star of tonight's show."

Sitting at the bar, Lexis replies, "Jennifer, everyone I talked to said that they will be here tonight."

Jennifer says, "We are completely booked up."

Lexis says confidently. "Candio and I are ready."

Sandy then says, "Jennifer, did you hear about what happened this morning?"

Jennifer points to the television.

"It's all over the news."

Noticing Zongzi's bloodshot eyes, Randy pats him on the shoulder.

"How's the harmonica-man feeling?"

Zongzi replies. "I'm hung over, freezing and brain dead. I feel like curling up by the fireplace."

Randy then says. "You mean, over there on that thick, fuzzy grizzly bear rug?"

Zongzi replies. "Don't temp me."

Getting up off the barstool, Randy walks over to the fireplace.

"I'll stoke the fire and warm this old place up."

While her husband attends to the fireplace, Jennifer says, "Any of you want something to eat?"

Zongzi quickly responds. "Nothing for me."

"No thanks. I 'm here to rehearse, but when you get a chance, Sandy and I, would like some coffee. We have a long day ahead of us." Lexis adds.

Jennifer fills two cups of coffee and brings them their steaming drinks.

"Enjoy." Jennifer says and then looks at Lexis. "Are you going to the remembrance service and movie?"

Lexis replies. "Sandy and I are going. Zongzi's going up to his room to sleep. Then after the movie, Dean wants us all to go to over to his house for the party. Ida and Lloyd said that they're going home after the movie. I am hoping they change their mind. Sandy and I might stop at the party, but, only for a little while. But, seeing the way the snow is coming down we might come straight here. I want to be ready for the contest."

Jennifer says. "Wish I was going to Dean's party. Rub elbows with those high society muckity mucks."

Zongzi interjects. "I bet that Lucy Leigh and Kelly Carlson will be there? They're smoking hot."

Jennifer adds. "Kelly's playing Janis in the movie. Gossip has it that Dean has a date with her."

Sitting down at the bar, Randy says. "A tabloid reported that Kelly used her looks to play Dean."

"Kelly Carlson's a slut. She is one of the reasons that I don't want to go the party." Lexis adds.

Sandy says, "Did you see Lucy Leigh in 'Bombs Away'?"

Lexis replies, "Yes, she was great. That movie had me at the edge of my seat."

Sandy says, "Did you see who is playing Detective Sentieri in the movie?"

Lexis answers. "Yes, Anthony Trevino, if I do go to the party, Dean promised me to introduce us."

"He's adorable. And he was so sexy in 'The Southerner'." Jennifer adds.

Randy says, "He's the same guy, who was the detective in Crawl Space. Now that was a great movie."

Lexis says, "I still can't believe that they got Julian Rinehart to play Dean."

"I guess he signed on because he found out that all the movie proceeds go to the victim's families. And that's why he did the movie for free. He usually gets twenty million a movie." Jennifer adds.

Lexis says. "Did you see him in the previews? He gained a lot of weight and grew that gnarly beard. He even looks like Dean."

Feeling sleepy Zongzi yawns, stretches out and carefully rests his head on the bar.

Seeing this, Randy says, "Harmonica-man is down for the count."

Jennifer looks at Lexis.

"After your performance can you help bartend tonight?"

"Sure."

Sandy says, "Jennifer, if you need help, I can work the tables."

Jennifer smiles at Sandy.

"That would be great. So, do you think the police are getting any closer to catching the killer?"

Sandy replies, "I think so."

Zongzi slowly stands and mumbles, "Excuse me. Going to my room. I think I 'm going to barf."

The drowsy man then walks to the staircase. Grasping the handrail, he slowly makes his way up the stairs.

Randy says jokingly. "It's only a quarter to nine in the morning. Why did he even get up today?"

Sandy replies. "Zongzi's not a morning person. Most likely you'll soon hear strange noises coming from his room. When he's dreaming, he has been known to toss and turn a little. So, I brought some homemade wine to help him sleep soundly." Sandy giggles before she continues to say, "One time I saw him asleep and he had his lips puckered making bubble-like sounds. When he woke up, he told me that he had a dream where his spirit had taken refuge inside of a gold fish."

Lexis interjects. "Sandy told me one time that Zongzi was sleepwalking and he walked right off the end of a pier."

"You should have seen the look on his face when came up out of the water." Sandy says giggling.

Superman's on the way

Dressed in a sharply pressed pinstriped navy-blue suit and black overcoat, Detective Sentieri walks out the door. Carrying a small cage, he walks to a rusty two-door silver sedan. He opens the car door, places the cage in the backseat and then climbs in. He puts the key in the ignition and turns the key. The cold battery begrudgingly turns the engine over. Feathering the gas pedal, the engine sputters and starts. While the engine warms up, he leans back and lights a cigarette.

"Ah the old car smell, can't beat it."

Taking a puff off the cigarette he waits for the engine to warm up.

Okay, what are the facts. Dean is cleared by way of DNA. The horrific forensic evidence shows that the killings we're personal. All the victims were raised in the same neighborhood. They all were living very productive lives and their futures were bright. Were the killers resentful of the victims promising lives?

After a few minutes, the detective puts his car in gear and heads down a parking ramp. Hearing his cell-phone ring, he eyes the incoming phone number.

Recognizing the number, he answers the call. "Hey bro, how's everything up there in Moon Lake."

At the lodge, sitting at the bar drinking coffee Randy replies, "It was windy earlier, but now the snow's really coming down."

Leaving the parking garage, the detective says, "It's raining here. But it's got to be going crazy up there."

"Reporters are everywhere. And, did you hear about what happened today? The killer struck again and left a body in an alleyway. They're haven a press conference soon."

"Where's Dean?"

"He's ice-fishing."

"Okay, I'm on my way."

"Hey Rob, you won't believe this, tonight Charlene's talent show is broadcasting live tonight. It's been ten years, but do you remember her?"

"Yes, I do. We were watching her sing, 'He loves to make me cry', when I got the call to go investigate the crime scene at the Unicorn."

"Charlene has come a long way since then. People from all over the world will be watching her show tonight. So, you should come and check it out. Tonight's going to rock!"

"Randy, that's cool bro. But make sure that you save me a bungalow. I'm going to be beat, and I do not want to sleep in the storage room again. Oh yea, when I get into town, I'm going to drop off my cat."

Seeing more people come into the lodge, Randy says, "I'm kind of busy. But, don't worry about it. I'll set up a litter-box."

The detective then hangs up and makes a phone call.

"Hello homicide. Can I help you?"

"Hello, this is Detective Sentieri can I…"

Before the detective can finish, the dispatcher quickly says, "Yes sir, I am re-directing your call."

A voce then answers and says. "Hey Rob when will you be in town?"

The detective recognizes the voice and replies, "Jack, I 'll get there as fast as I can."

"I'd like to meet with you soon as you get in. We've set up the Central Command Post in the second-floor conference room."

"Has the taskforce made any headway?" The detective inquires.

"Since today's discovery of a macerated body, we've established a one-hundred-mile perimeter. We've set up roadblocks and we've contacted law enforcement officers in the surrounding counties. We believe it is the remains of Gildardo Madrid. His wife and him have been reported as missing."

The detective responds. "You know that the victim is from the same neighborhood as the others?"

"Yes, and there is also evidence that the victim's wife was abducted at the crime scene. A note was found in the alleyway that matches previous notes. A forensic linguist has confirmed that the note was written by the Shoestring Strangler."

Before the detective hangs up the phone, he says. "Okay Jack, I have to stop at the theater first. But I'll see you as soon as I can."

Seeing that the rain is blurring his vision, the detective turns the windshield-wipers on high. Approaching a busy intersection, to prevent his vehicle from losing traction, he pumps the brake lightly to slow down. Pulling up to a stop-sign, in order not to slide on the road, he presses gingerly down on the break. At the intersection a school crossing-guard walks out in the street holding a stop sign.

As scarf faced children step briskly cross the street, Rob reminisces about his daughter; *I wish I'd been around more while she was growing up.*

He sighs, "I wish she would call me."

Interrupting his thoughts his cell-phone rings, he activates the ear speaker and says, "Hello."

A female voice says seductively, "Miss me?"

"Knowing it's you on the other line. Hearing your voice is breath of fresh air. Vicky, you're just what the doctor ordered."

"So, does that mean you've been thinking about us?"

"I 've had a lot on my mind. But I would like us to get together."

"It's been a while. When are you coming to Moon Lake?"

"I am on my way. So, how's the new job? Bet you're the sexiest news reporter in Moon Lake."

"Channel Six is a great. It's challenging but I work with a lot of very talented people."

"Yea and they're all looking at you. Has your boss asked you out yet?"

"No, but he wants me to ask you for a favor. Dean Stein wouldn't give me an interview. And so, the producer was wondering if I could interview you. I'm kind of getting pressured to ask you some tuff questions about the first investigation."

Because the intersection is clear, a car behind the preoccupied detective honks their horn franticly.

He sighs. "I can't wait till all this is over. Tell your boss I'll do the interview and I'll see you tonight."

"Okay call me later."

"Okay I will."

Stressed, the detective hangs up the phone and turns the radio on. After a few more intersections and stop lights, he turns onto the onramp of the freeway. Speeding up to merge on the interstate, a song comes on the radio.

Thinking about his rendezvous with Vicky, he sings along. "You're always on my mind."

Driving down the interstate, He lusts for her embrace. Smiling, he reminisces caressing her soft skin.

Obligated, the detective restrains his thoughts and refocuses on the case.

What's with that signature? Is it a way to taunt us? What a Hancock.

However, before he can think another thought, his cell-phone rings. Noticing that the rain has turned into snow, he steadies the steering wheel before he activates the ear speaker.

Answering the phone, the detective says, "Hello."

"Robbie how's the weather?"

"Hi mom. The weather is fine. How are you feeling?"

"I'm okay. Happy birthday son, your brother and I were talking about your twenty-first birthday party. Remember? You tumbled down the stairs holding a beer and brat? You lost the beer but held onto the brat."

"I remember very little of that night."

"How does it feel to be forty-three? Have you been taking your blood pressure pills?" Hearing Rob mumble incoherently she insists. "Have you?"

"Sorry mom, I didn't hear you. The roads are icy and this idiot in front of me is driving all over the place."

"Calm down, I'm just worried about you. Your dad had his heart attack when he was forty-three. So, you need to follow your doctor's advice to the letter."

"I am. But this restricted diet is killing me."

Announcing another incoming call, the phone beeps.

"Ma, I have another call. We'll talk later."

"Make us proud and catch this killer. I love you."

"I love you."

The detective activates the incoming call. "Hello, this is Detective Sentieri, can I help you?"

"Hey, you good for nothing piece of shit. Did you get your birthday card?"

"Yes, thanks. So, have you heard from our daughter?"

"Lori hates me because I left you. I haven't seen her since she walked out of rehab. You are the one who let her do what she wanted. She is your problem now. I called you because Ida told me that Lloyd has been taking care of the house. I drove by yesterday and he was shoveling the sidewalk. You know he has bad heart. I can't believe you let him do that. Then again, I guess it doesn't surprise me because you only think about yourself. They don't deserve a neighbor like you. And, I need some money to pay off the rehab center."

Cringing, the detective replies. "I don't have a penny in my pocket. Remember? The divorce, you got all the money and I got the house. So, I'm meeting with the bank tomorrow to see how much I owe in back taxes. Then, I'm going to see if I can sale the place."

Raising her voice, the woman replies. "Cheap bastard. I'm so glad I don't live in that shit-hole of a town!"

"After I settle with the bank, I'll call you."

"If you weren't so obsessed with pretending to be a detective, Lori wouldn't be so screwed up!"

The calls ends.

Frustrated, Rob grimaces as he continues to drive down the snowy interstate.

Unlucky Souls

Rapt in terror sitting in the dark, damp room, Martha feels around on the ground. Her hands come across a paper bag. She opens it and pulls out two smaller bags. She also pulls out a plastic bottle. Sitting against the wall, she unscrews the cap and takes a drink. The taste of cool water calms her. Sitting with her back against the wall, anxiety seeps into her bones. She resists the visions of her husband's nightmarish fate.

Like a pendulum, reality slashes deeper and deeper into her mind.

"The last thing I remember, holding onto Gildardo's arm and walking into the alley. Everything was going great. With grandmother there to take care of our little Martha, Gildardo and I could work overtime. We're caught up on our expenses and we finally have some money in the bank."

Trying to think of a happier moment, Martha remembers when Gildardo had first revealed his dream of coming to America.

"He looked at me with his big eyes full of hope and said, 'In America our family will have a better chance for happiness'."

She reminisces on how happy they were when they bought their house. When they first moved into it and how they filled it with memories. Ambushing her tender thoughts, the dark cloud of her childhood fills her with sadness.

Searing memories of abuse surface from the darkness of her mind; *Mother said that she wished that she had never given birth to me. She never needed a reason to beat me. When I told her that I was molested by father, she called me a liar and to kill myself for being such a burden. She made me sit on a bucket inside the hallway closet. By the grace of God, I found comfort by listening to the melody of the spirit.*

Martha sighs and whispers, "Gildardo, where are you." Feeling light headed Martha lies down and says herself. "How am I going to get out of here?" She then folds her arms over her stomach, closes her eyes and whispers. "God please help me."

Looking in the mirror brushing her hair Judy thinks; *I can't make up my mind, should I wear a dress or jeans. And where the hell is Richard? He told me that he'd be home in twenty minutes. I guess I need more time anyways. I'm surprised that his boss is letting him off early. Why worry, I'm sure that there's plenty of people there helping to get things ready. Oh, before I forget, I better call Ida to remind her to bring Shannon's photo album.*

Judy then picks up the phone and dials but there's no answer. *I guess I can send her a text.*

After sending the text message Judy dials another number.

"Good morning, this is Jennifer. Can I help you?"

"Hello Jennifer, is Lexis there?"

"Hold on a second?" Jennifer finds a place to set down the coffeepot. When she returns to the phone, she says, "Sorry about that, lots of things going on. They're setting up cameras for the live television broadcast. I have a group here for lunch and I have a big pile of fish to fry."

"Your fried fish is the bomb. Better fry up two piles."

"Yea right. All we want is for everyone to have a good time. Hold on and I'll give the phone to Lexis, she's rehearsing." Jennifer quickly walks over by the stage and hands the phone to Lexis.

"Hello, this is Lexis."

"What's up Lex. Are you ready for tonight?"

"Jude, I'm so nervous. I guess that people from all over the world will be watching tonight."

Judy replies. "You're going to be a star. I can't wait to see the new act. What are you going to wear?"

"We're both wearing black tuxedos, red bowties and red leather boots."

"Wow, dressed for success. Sorry to interrupt you. But, remember you're helping me with the eulogy. I'm depending on you."

"I've known you since third grade, have I ever let you down?"

"No, you haven't that's why I love you too death."

Judy then says goodbye, pours herself a glass of chardonnay and sits down in the living-room.

Sipping the wine, she thinks to herself; *Time does fly. The first vigil held at the theater, now that was tough. I didn't know how we'd ever get through it. Especially, when some kids chanted, "Lexis's the Moon Lake maniac." Come to think of it, there are still some people who think Lexis is the killer. Shannon and Lexis had some pretty heated arguments. They did not like each other at all. But that doesn't mean she would kill her own sister.* To pull her mind out of the past, Judy turns on the television.

She takes another sip off the glass of wine and says to herself, "Looks like I have just enough time to catch up on my soap and have another glass of chardonnay. Then off to the remembrance."

Inside the snow-covered shanty, holding a cup of soup, Dean's thoughts drift back in time.

Watching the steam rise from the cup of hot chicken broth he whispers, "I can't believe it's been ten years."

He thinks about his book and what he wrote; *Seven unlucky souls came to watch a show. Now, their body parts are scattered leaving only a bloody torso. Propped up in the front row and around their neck is a shoestring neatly tied in a bow.*

Dean rubs his face and flounders over the misery of what he went through writing the book.

Thinking out loud he says, "It did help me to deal with the reality that will sit on my chest for the rest of my life." Trying to cope with the tortuous recall, he envisions having dinner with Janis earlier on that tragic night. A tear forms and runs painfully slow, down his cheek. "She was wearing her favorite shirt. The one with a pink pig with wings. Oh yea, she also wearing those sexy tight jeans." Dean looks across the fishing hole at the panting dog. "Tobias, Janis made fried chicken that night. Just the way I like it. The chicken was nice and crispy, covered with mushroom gravy. It was just the two of us."

Deans pauses before adding, "I'd give anything to share that table with her again."

The dog looks back with hungry eyes and barks.

Dean responds by tossing the dog a piece of jerky. "You know, that was our last moment together. By the time we had finished eating, everyone in the neighborhood had shown up. Then, we all went out to the garage to listen to the band practice. They had this new song called, 'Blowing with the breeze'. They were scheduled to play it the following night at the high school. Tobias, I always wondered about that fact. Were they murdered because they were so talented? When they finished practicing, we all went to the theater. Back then, I was the janitor so while everyone watched the movie, I cleaned the place." Before continuing, Dean grimaces as he sips the steamy chicken broth. He looks back at the dog and says, "When the police first woke me up. I didn't know what the hell they were talking about. It felt like I'd been drugged or something. I told them, but they didn't believe me. They called me a monster, handcuffed me and then showed me what had happened. It felt like I was living a nightmare. There was so much blood. Then they took me to the police station and kicked me around. They really put the screws to me. I couldn't take anymore. So, I said yea, I strangled the only woman that I've ever loved." Dean looks up and sighs as tears runs down his face. He wipes the tears away and looks at the dog. "Tobias, I wanted to kill myself because I didn't want to go on without her. And I watched those kids grow up. I loved them like they were my own. But the police wouldn't listen. And, they would not stop until they got me to confess to something I could never do."

The dog tilts his head and whimpers.

"They looked at me just like that. And Toby, I'm not crazy. I'm telling you they ruffed me up. When they were done, they threw me in the wacko ward!"

Dean leans back and wiggles the fishing line. "I should sue them."

To ease his mind, his thoughts carry him back to simpler times. Before the gruesome murders.

Moon Lake was a place where people built there summer cottages. Everyone knew everyone. People were friendly. Nobody locked their doors. People would come up here just to get away from the rush of city life. Now, there's tourist poking all around. All they want to talk about is the Shoestring Strangler

Finishing off the cup of broth Dean places the cup back on top of the thermos.

He looks back at the dog. "Toby, it's been ten years to the day since my lovely wife was taken from me. Our memories have helped me to get though the pain of missing her."

Reality fades as Dean's mind nestles comfortably into the caressing memories of the past.

Lift off

On stage at the lodge, Lexis rehearses as a woman arranges tripods around her. Wearing navy blue slacks and a long sleeve gray shirt she adjusts the lights on top of the tripods. Positioning the light to shine on Lexis, she thinks; *She's really working hard.*

She then hears Lexis say something and is about to answer her when he sees that she has her ear-buds in.

She must be talking to someone

Hearing her stomach moan, she walks over to the Jennifer behind the bar. After watching her dump out a batch of freshly fried fish, she says, "Excuse me, can I try a piece?"

Using a paper towel, Jennifer hands her a piece.

"Watch out Char. It's hot."

"During the TV broadcast, I'm going to tell the world about your fried fish." the woman replies.

Back in the adjoining room, a group of people sit at a table sipping hot tea.

Watching Lexis rehearse, a man at the table says quietly, "She seems very sure of herself. That doll is a very realistic. It seems to be looking right at me."

Also, in a quiet tone of voice, a woman at the table say, "Have you tried the cinnamon honey tea? It's so good."

Another woman then says, "Do you recognize that woman at the bar?"

The man replies. "Yep, that's Charlene. She was singing here the night of the Unicorn massacre."

Finished eating, Charlene walks back near the stage. She looks through a camera and focuses in on Lexis.

Adjusting the camera, she says quietly, "Tonight, a star is born."

Sitting in the bar area talking to Jennifer, Sandy overhears someone say, "Something special is going to happen here tonight. I can feel it in the air."

Sandy walks over by Jennifer and says. "I'm getting a dose of déjà-vu. I'm going to check on Zongzi."

Sandy then gets up, walks back through the stage area, past the fireplace and up the stairs. When she makes it to the second floor, she walks down the hallway.

Talking to herself Sandy says, "Jennifer said that he's in room seven."

Reaching the room, Sandy opens a door to find Zongzi sitting with legs crossed and eyes wide open. Approaching him, she stretches out her arms and slowly moves her fingers in the air. She kicks her leg high and dances toward Zongzi. To emanate peaceful vibes, she places her hands over him and wiggles her fingers. Satisfied with what she feels in her gut she concludes that he's ready. She then tilts his head back and massages his temples. She can see his eyes twitching back and forth. Realizing what he's up against, a sharp pain twists in her heart.

She whispers, "Zongzi put your pride aside. Rise above the cloud of revenge and hate. Find the passion and allow love to fill your soul. Be lifted up into the realm of tranquility. Seek and find out what we need to know. Become one with the truth. Become the dream sleuth." Generating positive vibes, she calmly adds, "Zongzi, it's time for the preflight swig? Get ready to do your dreamscape jig?"

Zongzi's eyes go still and he answers her by pointing to a suitcase on the bed. Sandy walks over to the suitcase and pulls out two green bottles. She places one on a night stand near the bed. She takes the other bottle and sits beside Zongzi.

Handing the bottle to Zongzi, she says, "Let love shoot through the heart. Rise above the masquerade and just be who you are."

"Sandy, I'm ready."

"Now where's that gothic corkscrew?" Sandy asks.

Zongzi holds up a tarnished corkscrew.

"Here it is."

He then twists the corkscrew's pigtail into the cork and slowly pulls the cork out.

When the bottle pops, Sandy says, "Chug-a-lug dreamscape slug."

Zongzi takes a healthy drink and tries to hand the bottle to Sandy.

She refuses it.

"It's all for you the dream sleuth. Slam it down and slip into the truth."

"It has a very familiar aroma. What's in this batch? It is making my heart race?"

Listening to Zongzi Sandy's eyes widen.

She then replies, "It's my mid-summer's eve, juniper berry wine, topped with a dash of powered white rose peddles and thyme."

Zongzi eyes widen in anticipation as puts the green bottle to his lips. He raises the bottle as the mystic potion continues to rush down his throat. With every swallow his inhibitions bubble into the air and his spirit disconnects from his body. Almost instantly his throat thirsts for more. He tilts the bottle higher for more of the psychedelic concoction.

Sandy's voice becomes distorted and sounds like if she is speaking in slow motion.

"To thwart demonic spirits who creep on their tiptoes, I've sprinkled a few drops of wine on your pillows. And so, your thoughts do not get eaten by locus, I've placed holed stones on your headboard to keep your path in focus. Inside your pillowcase there's a dried right eye of a cod that will ground you like a lightning rod."

Before he can say anything, Sandy hands him an apple.

She then says, "You must sleep with this to keep you from going insane. This apple will ward off demons who want to devour your brain."

Holding the apple and sensing her dire urgency, Zongzi continues to drink the bottle. The bouquet of sweetness incites his tongue. After a few more swigs the bottle is dry. He notices how the walls of the room have become vibrant rainbows.

Realizing that Zongzi is feeling the effects of the potion, Sandy gets up and walks to the door.

Zongzi raises the empty bottle up to his eye. Like a periscope, he peers through the bottle and watches Sandy walk out the door.

Looking through the bottom of the bottle, he whispers, "I've drank the booze there's no time to lose."

Zongzi then lies down on the bed and puts his sleepy head on the pillow.

Sandy waits just outside the door.

She whispers to herself. "Don't wait, do what it takes to stop this killing. Keep thoughts moving forward and trust your instincts. If something doesn't feel right, distance yourself from it. Don't be caught up in the self-indulgent cesspools. To find out who the killer is, you must reconnect with the universal truth. Sidestep the ballyhoo and slip into the grove." As she speaks premonitions flash in Sandy's mind and she adds. "Zongzi, the flesh is too weak to understand. It is the spirit's destiny to rise above the flesh and return to the Creator's hand." Knowing how emotions could compromise his dreamscape, Sandy gets controls of her thoughts. "There's not a second to waste so be on your way."

Back inside the room Zongzi breathes deep and his mind goes blank.

Inducing a trance Sandy begins to sway back and forth.

She wiggles her fingers at the door of Zongzi's room.

Using a monotone voice, she chants. "Be carried away in the arms of Love. Up into the blinding Truth above."

With a sinking feeling rolling in Zongzi's stomach, his body becomes increasingly vexed.

Sandy continues. "We've opened our hearts and cried. We've overtook loss and survived." Trying to drain the suppressed tension deep within the sleepy truth seeker, she calmly whispers. "From out of the crucible of Love may you be immersed and dispersed to every corner of the universe."

Zongzi then begins to feel lightheaded. His skin tingles and his body twitches. He babbles incoherently.

Hearing this. Sandy puts her hand over her mouth and prays; *Cleaned, enriched, within the warm sunshine, lift Zongzi to the place where there are only rhymes. Time will cease to be, on the count of one, two and three.*

With these words, Zongzi feels his spine twitch and his spirit tingles as it slips out of his body. Walking away from his flesh, he feels a sharp pain from the back of neck. He turns to sees a strand of light that stretches from the back of his neck to his body. The tension eases the further he walks away. In wonder, he looks at Sandy standing on the other side of the door. He can taste her anguish.

"There's no need to worry, I'll find out who the killer is."

Zongzi's thoughts fade into nothingness. His spirit shoots up into a funnel of golden light. The blazing light soothes his nerves. Vicious and decisive winds hone his flailing spirit. The Light becomes focused and begins to fill his spirit. Like a balloon, his spirit stretches out until it dramatically bursts. Zongzi's life essence splashes out in waves of golden dust that shimmer silently to all corners of the universe.

Stick to the plan

In the bar area of the lodge, watching television, people chew on breaded pieces of cod.

"Good Morning Moon Lake. This is Lou Trudeau and welcome back to Channel Six's special news report. There has been a diabolical development. Earlier this morning, in proximity of the Unicorn Theater, a dismembered body was discovered in an alleyway. Already the police department's hand writing expert has confirmed that the note, discovered at the crime scene, was written by the Shoestring Strangler. Hold on, breaking news to follow, an impromptu news conference has just ended at police headquarters. To sum it up for us, broadcasting live, here is Vicky Marcus."

Pressed between news-reporters clamoring around her, the camera lens tries to focus in on reporter's grim face.

The woman looks into the camera. "I am here at the Moon Lake police department and before our news camera came online, Moon Lake's Chief of Police, handed the briefing over to the FBI, Task Force Commander, Jack Mahoney. Agent Mahoney then confirmed that the Shoestring Strangler's carnage has taken another life." Looking down, reading from her memo pad, she continues, "It occurred today in the alleyway near the Unicorn Theater. According to forensics, using body temperature to gauge, the death occurred between seven-thirty and seven-forty-five AM. The Medical Examiner has ruled it a homicide. The ME confirmed that the victim died as a result of affixation byway of strangulation. And the dismemberment was carried out after the victim had expired. Agent Mahoney tried to calm the reporters by saying, Moon Lake has over one hundred law enforcement officers on the job. When he was finished addressing the crowd, one reporter shouted out, 'why is the Mayor endangering lives by not canceling local events?' Agent Mahoney adamantly replied, 'we've set up live surveillance cameras inside the Unicorn Theater and when the weather lets up, we're launching drones. These drones will have a live feed to the taskforce command center.' He went on to assure that the residents of Moon Lake are safe. This is Vicky Marcus for Channel Six News. Back to you Lou."

Inside Norma Genes All Night Dinner, a woman gets up from the counter and walks to the bathroom.

Still sitting at the counter, a demented mind ponders; *The FBI is doing what I expected. What simpletons. When they look back at their decisions, they'll regret trying to outthink me. And if Moon Lake likes the movie just wait until they see the sequel. Now let's get back on schedule. Who's next on the list? Oh, how could I forget the little redheaded whore? Where she's at?* A hand reaches out and picks up a cell-phone. A finger pokes out a telephone number.

A voice comes from the phone. "Hello, Channel Six Tip Line, can I help you?"

Trying to disguise his voice, he speaks using a high pitch, "Yes, I have information on the Shoestring Strangler. But I want to be interviewed by Ms. Marcus. Is there any way she could meet with me?"

"Please give me your name and address."

"I want to remain anonymous, is she's still at the police station?"

"If you hurry, you can catch her there."

"I'm not even dressed. But I could be ready in a few minutes. Can I meet with her a little later?"

"When Ms. Marcus is finished at the police station, she will be going to Moon Lake Cemetery. Then she will be covering the Remembrance at the theater."

"I should be able to catch her at the theater. Thanks for the info."

Coming back from the bathroom a young woman sits at the counter.

She looks at the cell-phone and says. "There you are. I thought I'd lost you?"

Looking back at the counter, with a conniving grin, the bells jingles as he walks out the dinner's door.

The twisted fiend then whispers, "I'm heading for the cemetery, this is going to be easy. When Sentieri finds out, his head will be so screwed up. And, while the dumb-ass bangs his head against the wall, I'll execute the God's plan."

Rehash the past

Snow flings off the tiers as Detective Sentieri drives down the interstate. Gazing at the oncoming white landscape the detective turns off the radio. The motion of the windshield-wipers and the constant hum of the motor capture his mind. A brief moment of relaxation passes before a sick feeling begins to twist in his gut.

I can't get it out of my head. Strangulation and dismemberment, makes it personal. The only similar case of dismemberment was back when I was a rookie. I was working in Dodge County. A resident called in a report of an animal carcass in the middle of the road. On arrival at the scene, it was evident that they were human remains. There was thick dark blood pooled around the mangled human torso. The trailing blood splatters showed that it had been rolled or dragged down the street by a vehicle. With no eyewitnesses and no tire tread prints found at the scene, the investigation quickly went cold. Then, more severed human body parts were uncovered at the local landfill. A few days after this discovery a call came in from a concerned citizen. They had called to complain about a pungent smell coming from a street sewer. The sewer was in the same area of the torso that was found. When investigating, I looked down into the sewer and found more human remains. The rotting flesh was white, and maggot infested. After we had unclogged the sewer pipe, we followed it. The pipe led to the residence of a very attractive woman, who introduced herself as Molly. I had seen her prior to that working at the butcher shop. When confronted, she nonchalantly admitted that she had flushed the body parts down the toilet. She also calmly informed me that there were more bodies stored under the floorboards in her living room. While the coroner removed two bodies from beneath the wooden slats, I searched the residence. Following a foul stench, it led me to the hallway closet. When I opened the door, I found a charred human torso inside of an aluminum bag. Then, as I continued to search, I noticed a fire pit smoldering in a field behind the residence. I quickly got a hose and put the fire out. When it cooled, several human skulls and a pile of charred bones were collected. These and other genetic fragments were later identified by forensics to be human remains. And, when I questioned Molly about it, she told me how she'd lure her victims to her house. She said, 'I was answering their prayers. I'd go to a bar and look for lonely and depressed souls. Then, I'd go over and asked them if they needed a friend. They'd look me in the eyes and that's all it took. All they wanted was a place to call home and I gave them one. The hardest part was getting rid of them. So, when they'd pass out from drinking, I'd strangle them and store their bodies beneath the floorboards. Then, after a few days, their bodies would loosen up. That's when we would dance. Or, I'd prop them up in the chair and socialize. Sometimes, we'd play dress-up and have parties.' She also, nonchalantly, informed police that she had lost count of how many people she had, in her own words, 'Set free from misery'. By the end of the investigation, Molly's house had one more secrete to reveal. Searching the attic for clues, I found three young girls hiding behind some boxes. When I questioned Molly about the girls, she stated that on a cold winter's night she heard a knock at the door. Then, when she opened it, she found the children on the doorstep. Thinking it was a gift from God, she happily decided to raise them as her own. Today Molly sits in the state penitentiary. This this the only familiar case with dismemberment in the county. And here is the direct connection. All three children who were found in the attic were adopted by couples from Moon Lake. The oldest of the girls, Shannon was adopted by Ida and Lloyd. Pricilla was adopted by Norma Gene. Lexis was adopted by Janis and Dean. Considering that Shannon was a victim of the Shoestring Strangler, are these crimes interconnected? Could Lexis and Pricilla be connected? Ida and Lloyd did say that when they first got Shannon that she told them that she had an older sister. I found no evidence to support that. One fact can't be overlooked. In contrast, to the Molly dismemberment case, the Shoestring Strangler is not your usual psychopath. How could a psychopath this deranged remain dormant for so many years? Another blaring fact about this investigation. Whoever is responsible for the slayings must be in great physical condition. The crime scenes are too complex. The surgical debauchery is too precise and personal. Disturbing his train of thought, from the back seat the kitten meows.

"I know you're hungry. It's not much further."

A hand to hold

Handing his wife an onion, Randy hears the door of the lodge open. With snow blowing at their back, a group of people hustle inside. Once inside the foyer, they stomp the snow off their feet and take off their coats. After gawking at the stuffed grizzly bear and other hunting trophies they walk into the lodge. Behind the bar, Jennifer cuts up the onion while Randy throws beef ribs on the grill.

In the adjoining room up on stage, Lexis arranges her stage props neatly inside of a suitcase. After zipping up the suitcase she sees Sandy come down the stairway.

"Is Zongzi asleep?"

"Yea, he's in a deep sleep. How did rehearsal go?" Sandy says.

"I've been waiting for this opportunity all my life. My mind's racing and I'm very nervous. But, I'm ready"

Lexis then puts her suitcase backstage and they both walk into the foyer. They put on their winter coats and leave the lodge.

After Lexis's car warms up, they drive down the snowy road. Not far down the road they park outside a house. The door of the house opens, and a couple walks out and towards the car. Watching them walk to the car Sandy says. "How long have Ida and Lloyd been married?"

"Over fifty years." Lexis replies.

When the elderly couple are in the car, Ida says, "Thanks for picking us up." She then reaches over and takes hold of Lloyd's hand. "Lloyd wanted to drive, but our car is terrible in the snow."

The conversations are light as they drive to theater. When the marquee comes into view, like a turnbuckle, the moment twists in Lloyd's gut. A crowd of reporters and cameramen surrounds the car.

Lloyd says, "Who are all these people? Why can't they just leave us alone?"

Getting out of the car Lexis notices that Lloyd is carrying the photo album and says, "Lloyd, after I serve the food can I look at Shannon's album?"

"Yes, we'll look through it together."

On the way into the theater time seems to slowdown for Lloyd. Faces distort, and their words become muffled. He can feel his heart pound as he reaches out to take hold of his wife's hand. Ida feels his pain. "Honey, we'll get through this. Remember, today is the day we let go."

Seeing how crowed the theater is, Sandy says, "Lexis, do you need any help with serving the food?"

"Yes, looks like we'll need it."

Lexis and Sandy then walk to the tables of food as Ida and Lloyd walk towards the theater.

Ida and Lloyd pause to look at the flower arrangements before they continue into the theater.

From behind a table serving coffee and donuts, Sandy sees Judy waving to her.

Sandy walks up to her and says, "Hey Jude, are you the official donut tester?"

"Yes I am. And make sure you try one of Ida's Swedish cheesecake donut holes."

Judy looks at Lexis, "Did Ida bring the photos? I want to see all the old pictures. Especially the pictures of the parties at your house."

"Yea, Lloyd has it. He's probably sitting in the theater paging through it. Where's Richard?"

"He wanted to get away from this crowd. So, he's eating up in the projector room." Judy replies.

"Okay, I'll be right back. I got to ask him something. I'll be right back."

Lexis then quickly disappears into the crowd. Sandy joins Judy serving coffee and donuts.

Soul mending

Warming his hands over a small propane heater, Dean keeps an eye on the fishing line. Across the circular fishing hole, a thick furred German Shepard chews on a piece of jerky.
Envisioning all his friends at the remembrance, Dean decides to make a phone call.
Dialing the number, he thinks; *I'll call Judy to find out if everything is going as planned.*
Handing out donuts and coffee, Judy is happy to see all the smiling faces.
She thinks to herself; *It's nothing like the first memorial service. Everyone was in tears.*
Starting her, the cell-phone buzzes in her pants. She takes out the phone and recognizes the incoming number.
"Hey Dean, catch anything?"
"No, I'm just sitting here thinking about Janis. I bet the place is packed."
"You would not believe it. You know that Ida's going to be very disappointed that you're not here. She said that she'd made Swedish meatballs because she thought you'd be here. Are you coming?"
"I just don't want to be smothered by all those reporters. Tell Ida thanks for the chicken dumpling soup. And, tell everyone that I appreciate all sincere letters when I was in prison. I do feel really bad that I'm not there."
"Dean, can you hear that?"
"What?"
"I'm in the lobby and your uncle, the mayor, is bragging about your date with Kelly Carlson."
"Judy, that's another thing. I just don't know if I'm going to the première or the party. I just might stay out here."
"Well, I'm not going to pressure you. But remember that we all love you. Besides, with all the money you've gave to this community, you could be Moon Lake's next mayor."
"You think they're happy now, just wait till the money starts rolling in from the movie."

"Did you hear how much tickets for the première are going for?"

"Judy, the hype is ridiculous."

"Dean, I'm sorry, I have to go. We're starting, and I've got to cue the music."

"Okay Jude, we'll talk later."

Dean puts the phone down and turns on the radio.

As he jiggles the fishing line, a boisterous voice comes out of the radio. "Ka-Boink anti-fungal toenail creams will do the trick."

After a pause of silence, another voice says, "Welcome back to Moon's Lake's favorite radio station. Today, we're asking our listeners the big question, who is the Shoestring Strangler? So, let's see who is on the phone lines. Right now, we have someone on the phone who still thinks that Dean Stein is the Shoestring Strangler. Even with the DNA evidence that has cleared him, what makes you believe that he's the killer?"

In reply, a loud voice blurts out. "This ain't no fiddle-faddle. If you follow the money, it's obvious that Dean is the killer. He was the only one that could've done it. And that's that."

"What about the murder in Chicago and the DNA evidence?"

"With all the money Dean's family has, they could have paid someone."

"You mean someone to stage the murder and plant the DNA?"

"Yes!"

The radio announcer says. "I'm not going to jump on that train. But I have seen stranger things."

Feeling frustrated, Dean turns the radio off. "That's it. I'm calling in."

He then picks up his cell-phone and makes a phone call. When his call is answered, a voice says. "Who's calling please?"

"This is Dean Stein. I'd like to respond to the caller's accusations."

"Mr. Stein, I'll have to put you on hold for a just a second. But I'll get you on the air immediately."

While on hold, Dean can still hear the same caller theorize how he's the killer.

After the caller hangs up, the radio announcer says. "If you are just tuning in, welcome to Moon Lake radio and we now have Dean Stein on the line. Mr. Stein, does the previous caller deserve a response?"

Before he says anything, Dean takes a deep breath. "I just called to say, that I did not kill anyone. And, I want to thank everyone who visited, wrote and prayed for me while I was in prison. If you've ever been in jail, you know how much it's appreciated. You find out who really cares and what really matters in life."

The radio host says, "It must have been tough sitting in prison for something you didn't do."

"Yes, it was. Living with criminals was miserable. They're some that are trying to rehabilitate themselves. But there are some very sick minds. The only way they feel good about themselves is to verbally abuse others. Even at night you could hear their hateful words throughout the night. It got to the point where I wanted to pull my ears off."

While Dean leans back and checks his fishing line, the radio announcer says, "Go on."

"In jail, you quickly realize the simple things in life that are taken for granted. You miss the little things. It's a very humbling experience."

Realizing Dean is becoming depressed, the announcer replies, "How's the ice fishing? Catch anything?"

"Nothing worth mentioning, but thanks for taking my call."

"Mr. Stein, all day long people have been calling in and saying how you made Moon Lake proud. It's astonishing how you've turned a tragic thing into hard cash for the victim's families."

Dean says, "If you can't help your neighbors what good are you."

"Mr. Stein, I personally want to thank you for your donation to Hanson High. My son says that he uses the new weight room all the time."

Thinking he saw his fishing line jiggle, Dean says goodbye and pulls the line out of the icy waters.

Seeing the bait gone, he whispers, "The big one that got away."

He then reaches into the bait bucket and grabs a silver minnow. After sticking the fish on the hook, he sets it back into the water. Setting the pole down he puts his foot on it and warms his hands over the heater.

Gazing into the fishing hole Dean says, "Janis, I know I promised. But I don't think that I'm not ready yet."

The sad man turns the radio back on and listens as the voice says, "We'll get back to taking your calls at the bottom of the hour. But right now, here's a poem that is inscribed on the cover of the Remembrance program; 'I carry you in my soul where-ever I go. The memories of your life I tenderly hold. They shine in my mind like a beautiful rainbow. Feeling lost, missing you and your smiling face, I know you're in a higher place. A place, I pray one day we will again tenderly and forever embrace.'"

Somberly speaking, the announcer adds, "I like that poem. And now, we're going to play a violin solo performed by one of the victims of the Unicorn Massacre. Shannon, at the time of her passing, was a sophomore at Northland Pines High School. The song is Paganini caprice number twenty-four. This is her last known live recording."

Following his words elegant and lofty sounds of a violin fills the airwaves.

Listening to the song, with tears in his eyes, Dean looks at the dog. "That's some fancy fiddle playing."

Unforgettable

Walking across the stage of the Unicorn Theater, Judy waves to the crowd.

Reaching center-stage she faces the crowd and smiles. "I want to welcome everyone to today's remembrance. On this tenth anniversary, we gather to remember the ones who were murdered. The first speaker is the mayor of Moon Lake, Theodore Whitaker."

A burly man with thinning hair, dressed in a dark suit walks out to the podium.

He clears his throat, adjusts his round spectacles and looks out to the crowd. "Good afternoon and thanks for coming to support the families. In the beginning, in our despair, we have questioned God. Why couldn't He protect these lives from ending prematurely? Who knows? Maybe there are no words capable to be the answer. Let's be thankful for what God has given us from this tragedy. A deeper understanding of how love can help us through the darkest of days. And through this love our community has bonded even tighter. God's plan is always centered with love. And through love we'll rejoin our sisters and brothers. Then, we'll understand His glorious plan. However, we'll accept this truth and together move on. Today, with reverence, we'll reminisce about the ones whose lives have touched us all. We'll talk about the casual moments spent with them. We'll be astonished by the accomplishments of their shortened lives. But, mostly, and most certainly, we'll express how much we miss them. As you can see by all the support, we're fortunate to live in such a caring community. If you could look into the heart of this community, you would find Ida and Lloyd. This loving couple is always there to help anyone in need. Through the years they've held several grief support meetings at their home. Not only have they opened their home, they've opened their hearts. And Ida's Swedish meatballs have comforted our tummies." The mayor smiles and then rubs his stomach. "If you've haven't tried one, you'll get your chance. They'll be serving them out in the lobby when we're finished. They melt in your mouth. But for now, let's begin with remembering the victims who lost their lives ten years ago. Julie and Shannon made a very big impact on this community. They were both promising volleyball players. Together, these two best friends took first place at the regional doubles' tournament. They also had teamed up and donated their long hair to 'Locks of Love'. An organization who supplies free wigs for people battling cancer. Julie was very astute and had aspired to be a lawyer." Before continuing, the speaker takes another sip of water. The mayor then looks into Ida and Lloyd's eyes. "Shannon, the daughter of Lloyd and Ida, was extremely talented in everything she did. Who could forget the violin solo she played to a packed auditorium just days before her tragic passing. This virtuoso had already performed with the top orchestras across the country. Some successful people get caught up in themselves, Shannon wasn't one of those. In her spare time, she taught violin to children. And, one of her students will be performing at the conclusion of the ceremony."

A voice in the crowd shouts. "We miss you Shannon."

The speaker nods his head in agreement and continues. "Jose and Manuel are also missed by their parents and their eight siblings. Before they passed, these two young men were not the shy, quiet type. They both enjoyed singing and playing guitar. They were great entertainers. If you were feeling down, they'd always had a silly song that would lift your spirits. They were handsome and their band, The Moon Lake Jamboree, was very popular with the local teenage crowd. Two other musicians of this ensemble were Jason and John. Jason, played stand-up bass, John played keyboards and drums. These two best friends worked together at the theater. Between ripping tickets, working at the concession-stand and running the movie projector they kept very busy. Of course, they both enjoyed watching movies. And always ready with advice on which ones to see. The two close friends also shared other passions. Both were members of the high school track team. For such strong young men, they were very gentle and kind." The man then steps back from the microphone to take another sip of water before he continues. "To sum up Janis in a few words is not going to be easy. She was the most inspirational person I've ever met. She took it upon herself to take care of others and she was the heart and soul of this community. She was an angel of mercy. Janis was the oldest of the victims. At the time of her passing, she was thirty-four, recently divorced and raising a fourteen-year-old daughter. Janis headed various non-for-profit organizations. Her vision included charities like the Moon Lake Rummage Sale. This huge event is still held every July. It raises needed money for local charities. I cannot express how much this community misses her. She was like a mother to all the young adults of the neighborhood. She went as far as to allow The Moon Lake Jamboree to practice in her garage. We sadly miss all the victims. And this community wants to thank everyone for their support. Yes, we'll survive the heartache and the feeling of loss. These cherished smiling faces that have been stolen from our view are always in our hearts. May God give us the resilience to overcome challenges in our daily life." The mayor clears his throat, looks down at a note card and continues say, "Inside a theater named the Unicorn lives were strangled, ripped to be reborn. In that moment an angel welcomed them playing a golden horn. Announcing their arrival into the eternal. They are at peace with their soul's whole and not torn."

The mayor then folds his note cards and walks away from the podium.

Walking up to the podium, Judy says. "If anyone here would like to share anything, please feel free. Together, we can all mend."

Haunting facts

Driving down the snowy interstate, the detective envisions the bloody scene inside the theater where seven people were dismembered.

"The ghastly deeds were executed so swiftly. In such a way that it had to be more than one assailant."

Searching for suspects he acknowledges what he believes to be the most disturbing fact. The perpetrators live unsuspectingly in the Moon Lake community.

Being one of the few people who had investigated the Unicorn Massacre and the Chicago crime scene, he mentally compares facts; *Both murder scenes showed a vicious personal attack. Not only did all the victims grow up in Moon Lake, they grew up in the same neighborhood. What's make that neighborhood different from the rest?*

The detective checks his mirrors, signals and changes lanes. *Ten years ago, the first seven victims had gathered that night at the Unicorn Theater. They watched a private showing of a horror film.*

The detective's mind is bombarded with the morbid images of the slayings. However, no matter how upsetting it is to remember, he rehashes every detail.

The autopsy report concluded that the victims were drugged and strangled before their bodies were dismembered.

Gazing down the highway, he whispers. "What am I missing?" Remembering his therapy sessions. He breathes deep and says to himself. "Relax, let everything go. Let all distractions float farther and farther away."

His mind goes blank and he relaxes his grip on the steering wheel. The sound of the heater fan and windshield wipers numbs his mind. Like a balloon his head bobbles driving over a bump in the road. The detective's thoughts casually sink back into the past. He again pictures the ghastly scene inside the Unicorn Theater. Continuing to probe deeper into his thoughts, he sees bloody body parts and the bloody hand prints smeared across the white movie screen.

Not allowing his emotions to steamroll, the detective calmly reminds himself to stick to the facts. *Okay, start from the beginning. Judy Grayson, who works nights cleaning the theater, called at twelve thirty AM to report the crime. The seven victims found inside the theater were friends and who all grew up together. Forensics showed that the victims had expired around eleven PM. According to the autopsy, affixation by way of strangulation was the cause of death. To render the victims helpless, toxicology proved that they were chloroformed. Most likely before their limbs were bound with duct-tape. DNA signatures collected, from the pool of blood on the theater's stage, proved that all seven bodies were dismembered on the same spot. Blood cast off patterns showed that the body parts, as they were severed, were tossed from the stage. Then, each of their torsos, complete with head, were propped up in the front row seats. The killers left shoestrings neatly tied in a bow around their neck. Another fact is that there was no blood found on the shoestrings.* The detective sighs and shakes his head. "All that blood and no blood found on the shoestrings."

With his toes beginning to freeze the detective turns the heater fan from defrost to heat.

He again thinks to himself; *Dean, the janitor was found unconscious behind the concession stand. After he was revived, he didn't have any memory of what had happened. When taken into custody a note found was found in his pocket. It stated that it was 'by the will of our Holy God; and it was signed, 'Shoestring Strangler'. Inventory of the theater's crime scene showed no signs of forced entry. Nothing was missing. These accumulating facts prove that it wasn't a robbery, sexually motivated or a random act. The last time anyone had seen the victims alive was at seven-thirty. This was when they were seen on their way to the theater. The big breakthrough was when a new DNA signature was extracted from the duct-tape. After ten years this new evidence was enough to get Dean released from prison.*

Seeing a sign say that says, "Moon Lake Use Right Lane Only", The detective signals and then switches lanes.

His mind goes blank before he dives back into his thoughts; *When investigating the crime scene in Chicago, the window of opportunity was only twenty minutes. In this short time, the killer's bloody ritual entailed strangulation, dismemberment and the removal the victim's eyeballs. Not to mention a note stuffed in the victim's mouth. And a bloodless shoestring tied around the bloody torso's neck. But then, the first clue was recovered. A DNA signature was extracted from one of the eyeballs collected near the crime scene. Forensics imply that the killer chewed on the eyeball and spit it out. Surmising the gruesome details of the Chicago crime scene, it does show that the slayer's debauchery has escalated. The hand-written notes left at both crime scenes were confirmed to be written by the same person. They both stated that the slayings are to appease a higher power. Both notes were signed: "Shoestring Strangler". Instinctively the lone signature implies that the killer is working alone. But my instincts say otherwise. And facts don't lie.*

Needing to take a break, he turns on the radio.

Feeling like he going to bust out of his skin, the detective thinks; *Hope Randy saved me a room.* Recognizing the violin solo playing on the radio, the detective then thinks; *God only knows where Shannon would be if she was still alive.* With the snow fall increasing, the detective then turns the windshield wipers on high. *I wonder how's the remembrance is going?* His thoughts remind him about what haunts him the most. The anguish the victim's family members go through knowing that the killer is still out there.

The detective drives past a reflective yellow sign that reads, "Moon Lake Next Exit". Feeling drowsy from the long ride he turns onto the off ramp and drives carefully through the deep snow. Driving too fast for the snowy conditions, a red panel truck comes up from behind and passes him. Swerving in front of him, the inconsiderate driver honks his horn.

Distracting Rob from his frustrations, he shouts out. "What's your hurry?"

Feeling his blood boil, he tries to abort the frustrations of driving in bad weather.

A beep from his ear bud announces an incoming phone call. *Right on cue.*

Answering, he says, "Can I help you?"

A female voce responds desperately. "I am so sex starved I can't think of anything now."

"Vicky, I'll be at the lodge any minute. Going to drop off the kitten so we can meet there."

"I hate to wilt your plans. But, I'm at the cemetery right now. My boss wants a video of the all victim's grave markers. Can you believe that? Tom the cameraman is just about done. You remember Tom, Judy's brother."

Rob says. "Yes, I've known Tom for years. So, where are you going next?"

"Well, we also need shots of the Christmas decorations along main street. Rob, you should see the gravesite displays. They're heartwarming. But we're done here and we're loading equipment into the van. After we're done getting our shots, we're headed to the Remembrance to do interviews."

"Okay then I'll meet you at the theater. I'm not looking forward to seeing anyone, especially Ida and Lloyd. No one ever says anything about it but, I know that I remind them about how screwed up the original investigation went."

"Rob, I can't wait to see you. We are going out to celebrate your birthday. Maybe have some drinks."

Wanting to help load the van, Vicky tells Rob to be careful and she hangs up the phone.

Strangulation and abduction

A man with shoulder length black hair, puts a camera bag in the van. "Got the shots."

"Alright. Let's get the hell out of here. I hope there's hot coffee at the theater." Vicky replies.

Anticipating the warmth of the news truck, they hurry to load the van.

Close by, deranged eyes peer out from behind a large granite grave marker.

Transfixed by delusions and lust the stalker whispers, "Finally, they're getting ready to leave."

Behind the words, a tormented mind is exhilarated by a false sense of a heavenly purpose. Losing grip, good thoughts slip back down into a deep pit of selfishness. Like a rooster trying to stop the sun from rising, the stalker's moral compass goes haywire…

Driven by interwoven fallacies, a pair of hands clenches a shoestring like a garrote. Cloaked by self-serving righteousness, maniacal thoughts flip the switch to execute the plan. With breath rising in the cold air like an old steam train, the stalker slowly creeps up like a prowling cat.

Unsuspectingly, the cameraman opens the driver side door of the van. In one swift movement he is approached from behind. A shoestring is quickly pulled tightly around his throat. The man gurgles as he tries unsuccessfully to pull the shoestring away from his throat. The garrote digs deeper around his neck. His body goes into spasms as the attacker tightens the stranglehold. The strangler then viciously yanks the man to the ground. Feeling the victim expire the killer relaxes and enjoys a moment of solace.

Now incensed with ire the diseased soul swoops behind the unsuspecting female reporter. A maddening rage rips through the killer as he tries to subdue her. The reporter tries to stop the attacker from covering her nose and mouth with a moist piece of cloth. Unsuccessful, it doesn't take long for the chloroform to take effect and render her unconscious. The killer then picks her off the ground and carries her limp body to the back of the van. After placing the body in back of the van, the killer strokes her auburn hair. A soothing buzz pulsates through the fiend's veins as the killer's eyes roll afire.

Springtime rhyme

With the taste of sweet juniper dancing on his tongue, Zongzi falls into a deep slumber. With the help of Sandy's seductive potion his inner voice reminds him to focus on the mission. To find out who is responsible for the murders. The natural obligation of self-development is redirected to reconnect to the all-seeing Eye.

Instead of nurturing inadequacies Zongzi's subconscious sets out to find the truth. Being a connoisseur of Sandy's wine and tailored to be vigilant he is not mystified by these occurrences. Filled with serenity, by the feet his astral body is sucked up into a twisting vortex of bright white light. Trying to bring his surroundings into better focus, he rubs his eyes. The light is replaced by a starry night sky. He soon realizes that he is floating high above Moon Lake.

With snowflakes swirling around him, he thinks; *Why am I wearing red leotards?*

Stupefied, he ponders gazing down at colored blinking lights hung at the lodge. His nostrils flare as he breathes deep and calms himself. After a few breaths he begins to burp pink bubbles. Blue and yellow puffs of smoke percolate from out of his buttock. With every breath his spirit becomes more visible. During this transformation he is gently lowered down to the snowy lakeshore.

Watching the snow fall gently from the sky fills him with tranquility. Reaching the ground is feet sink into a snowdrift. He looks up, opens his mouth and tries to catch a snowflake on his tongue.

Looking up into the starry night sky, Zongzi says, "Look how big the moon is getting. It looks close enough to touch. Wow." He then admires a bright star that is moving slowly across the sky. It twinkles, shimmering high in the sky. The star begins to move faster falling from the sky. Faster and faster it falls closer and closer. The blinding, bright star grows in size and then splashes into the frozen lake.

Watching the ice shatter and water splash, he gets a gut feeling that he has seen this before. Looking back up he then sees the moon slowly disappear. The sun then quickly emerges from the horizon and fills the sky with light. Snowflakes melt in midair and a warm breeze engulfs him. The icecap on the lake also recedes and disappears. Zongzi looks into water and see lilies grow and blossom.

He is awestruck. A dumbfounded glaze washes over his face. Watching the lilies sway in the shallow water his mind goes blank. He then feels something push up in-between his toes. Looking down he sees light green buds sprout open. Within seconds he is surrounded by yellow and white daisies. Swept up in a wave of euphoria he struggles to defy the seductive urge of contentment. In a sleepy daze he again looks up to see the sun swing across the horizon. The sunshine quickly gives way to a bright full moon.

Sitting in the moonlight time slows down and Zongzi tries to refocus. Throughout the night he reminds himself about the killer's reign of terror.

Under a bright morning sun, Zongzi is bursting with fresh resolve. He gets to his feet, walks through a patch of fragrant wildflowers and toward the glassy lake. When he reaches the lake, he sticks his toes into the cool water.

Looking over the lake, he shouts. "The killer must be stopped!" Watching the breeze ripple the lake Zongzi hears something behind him. When he turns to look, he sees a gray goat come out of the bushes. The goat lowers its head and snorts. The skittish animal charges toward him. Zongzi quickly steps aside and the goat runs past him. The goat continues to the edge of the shoreline. With the sun glistening off the lake the goat begins to lap up the cool water.

The goat turns to him and smiles. In a gruffy voice the goat says. "Zongzi, I haven't seen you in such a long time."

Wondering how the goat knows him, Zongzi replies, "I'm trying to help find a killer."

The goat quickly replies, "No time to chitchat. There's a lot to do and see before you are at where you need to be."

Then, from behind, Zongzi hears a buzzing noise. He quickly turns around and sees a hummingbird zipping towards him. The tiny bird grazes the side of his head. In tune with the spontaneity of the moment, Zongzi's spirit leaps into the tiny bird's body.

Inside, as the hummingbird hops from flower to flower, Zongzi is invigorated by the bird's relentless passion for nectar. He hears the hummingbird's tiny voce sing, "Thanks for coming with me on my mid-day run. To drink sweet nectar drenched by rays of the sun."

Zongzi replies by revealing his conundrum to find out who is the killer is. However, when Zongzi is finished, there is no reply as the hummingbird continues to fly along the lakeshore. Zongzi tries again to stress the importance of his mission. However, the buzzing bird makes no acknowledgment that one word has been heard.

Recognizing the custom of talking in rhymes, Zongzi then says, "Please take me to where I need to be?"

In-between zipping from flower to flower the bird sings, "To see what you want to see may change reality. There's no race, no need for haste. Why ask who, what and why? The answers lie behind the eyes. Don't stumble or fumble to where you are going to. Open your heart, it's where to start."

The tiny bird beelines to a patch of flowers and spews the stowaway into a blossoming lilac. Existing only in essence, Zongzi is saturated by a golden mist. Savoring the sweet fragrance, he smiles. Within the darkness of his mind, a pair of eyes emerge and bounce toward him. The red eyes grow bigger as they bounce closer. When the eyes stop bouncing, he reaches out and touches what feels like a nose. Sensing that the animal wants to help him, Zongzi evaporates into the eyes.

Soon as he is inside the he realizes that it is a rabbit. Sensing the stowaway, the frantic bunny hops in a zigzag through the tall grass. Like a bull rider Zongzi holds on tight.

Self-actualization

Inside the theater on stage the high school's musical teacher shares her memories of the victims and their promising careers. When she is done, she walks off the stage. Next in line, a young man walks out to address the crowed theater. On his way to center stage he ponders; *I can't believe this. Came here trying to solve this senseless crime and now I'm learning the power of forgiveness. I have found compassion. I am so happy I came here.*

Reaching the podium, the man says, "Can you feel it?" The man opens his arms wide and smiles. "Today and here, I have learned that love is still alive. I am so relieved that my intense hatred for the Shoestring Strangler no longer grips my thoughts. The anger and frustration are gone. I will leave it to God."

Sitting in the front row, Ida squeezes Lloyd's hand.

The audience is mesmerized by the speaker as he continues to say. "Witnessing all the love here at this Remembrance Service has invigorated my soul! You see, my brother took his own life about a month ago. The way I saw it, because of drugs and alcohol, he was not in his right mind. Disgusted with himself, he thought that there was no way out. Because, he couldn't stand living his life the way he was, he took the permanent solution for his temporary predicament. The darkness of his mind didn't allow him to realize how love could set him free. I for one depended on his humor. When he saw that I was angry or just in a bad mood, he'd make it his business to make me laugh. To tune me into the moment and recognize that worldly matters do not mean a thing. Memories of his goofiness still help me through challenging moments. If I could say something to him, I'd tell him how special his memories are to me. I pray for him every day and thank God for giving me such a caring, insightful brother. Today, when I asked to say a few words your Mayor asked me if I would be the last speaker. He said that he wanted to end the personal testimonies with my message of hope. I agreed, and I am glad I did. Listening to all the people who knew the victims gave me more time to reflect. It opened my eyes to our resiliency. Our ability to overcome the loss of our most cherished love ones. The precious memories we shared with them open our eyes to the precious moment at hand. Tragedies bond us. I am so happy to share this moment with all of you. There's so much love in my heart at this moment."

Backstage, listening to the person speak, Judy thinks to herself; *Where's that poem?*

She checks her pockets and becomes frustrated.

She turns to Sandy and says, "Where's Lexis?"

"I haven't seen her since we got here."

Judy then sighs in relief, points and says, "Thank God here she comes."

Walking out of the backstage shadows Lexis says, "Did I miss anything?"

"Noticing that Lexis's wearing a different outfit, Sandy says, "Why did you change your outfit?"

"I had to. I went outside to smoke a cigarette, I slipped on the ice and ripped my shirt."

Seeing a sheet of paper in Lexis's hands, Judy says, "Is that the remembrance poem?"

Lexis nods her head and replies. "Yes."

"Where did you find it?"

"I guess something broke up in the projector room. And while I was outside smoking Richard came out and asked for a ride. I told him that I was already leaving to go home and change. So, I gave him a ride. While he was in the house getting his tool bag, he saw the poem on the refrigerator."

"Good." Judy says sighing in relief. She looks at Lexis. "You made it just in time, we're next. I'm going to say a few words about the recent victims, then you read the poem."

In the background the people in the theater clap and cheer as the last speaker walks off stage.

The reality of the moment twists in Lexis's gut, "I don't know if I can go through with it."

Judy reaches out and takes Lexis by the hand. The two women begin to walk out to the center of the stage. Trying to suppress the lump in her throat, Lexis tries not to look at the crowd. Feeling the eyes upon her the air thickens. Reaching the podium Judy lets go of Lexis's hand and pulls out note cards.

Looking down at the note cards Judy addresses the crowd. "Before we conclude today's remembrance, our community would like to thank everyone for their sympathies and prayers. After I say a few words Lexis will read a poem and then we'll hear one of Shannon's students play the violin."

Judy looks briefly at her note cards and says into the microphone, "I am going to start with mentioning the recent victims of the Shoestring Strangler. The first one is Jeffery Vaughn. His life was cut short last week. We all called him Spuds. He liked to play card games and video games. I remember watching him try to jump a park bench on his skateboard. He didn't make it and he tumbled hard on the concrete. But he got right up, tried again and eventually he made the jump. He liked to fish off the bridge and he always had a sly, impish grin stretched across his freckled face. His family and friends are heartbroken."

Judy chokes up for a minute and Lexis hands her a handkerchief.

Judy wipes her eyes and after a short pause she continues, "As we all know this morning, Gildardo was found slain and his wife, Martha, is still missing. This young couple, even though they work third shift, they'd find time to help out at the homeless shelter. Gildardo also made sure that after a big snow or extreme hot day, that the elderly in his neighborhood were safe and comfortable. This young loving couple and their family are in our prayers." Judy wipes the tears from corners of her eyes. "Nothing matters in this world except our relationships with one another. Let's face our challenges together knowing that they will make us stronger." Judy again wipes the corner of her eyes and steps back from the podium. Petrified Lexis steps forward to the microphone. She takes a deep breath to calm her racing thoughts. Remembering the victims, her body aches with deep sorrow. She imagines them all standing behind her on stage.

She clears her throat and looks down at the paper. She feels a tear roll down her cheek and sees it fall onto the paper. Watching the tear soak into the paper it smears some of letters of the poem.

From out of the corner of her eye she sees Judy next to her. Drawing strength from her Lexis puts her emotions in check. Determined to read the prayer, she pulls herself together. She looks out to the crowd and says. "I had a moment. But, I'm okay now." Lexis again looks down to the paper and begins to read:

"Remembrance Prayer:
Loving Creator, it's a pleasure to sing Your praise.
We ask that You nurture and guide us through our days.
You give us the strength and will to choose Your way.
Sheltered by Your blessings from above,
Protect us from evil, for we long to bask in Your love."

When Lexis is finished reading the prayer Judy steps up to the microphone. "Today is about remembrance and it is also about living to the fullest. This concludes our gathering. Thanks for coming and after the violin solo please join us in the lobby for food and refreshments."

Hand in hand, Judy and Lexis walk off the stage.

All eyes focus on a young woman who walks out carrying a violin. She looks up, points and then begins to play. Watching from the front row, Lloyd puts his arm around Ida. Listening to the violin solo their eyes fill with tears. While everyone listens to the melodic melody, news about a dismembered body found at the cemetery spreads through the crowd.

Forward

Biting onto the minnow, the fish pulls and tugs on the fishing line. Tobias barks and Dean responds quickly by setting the hook by jerking the fishing line. The dog scrambles to stand and begins to scratch the edge of the hole. The dog's long sharp nails scratch and scars the ice. With the fishing pole gripped in one hand Dean gets up and straddles over the fishing hole.

Trying to calm down the anxious dog, using a southern drawl Dean shouts, "Slop slapping your jaws."

While he eases tension on the fishing line, Dean lets the fish run.

He sits down and says, "Soon as I reel her in, you can skid-daddle!"

After several minutes Dean reels the fish in. He reaches back, grabs his net and scoops the fish out of the water.

"Now that's a muskie!"

Dean then takes hold of the fish and sing a pair of pliers, he removes the hook. After admiring the large fish, he then places it in plastic cooler. Tobias pokes his snout in the cooler and nudges the flopping fish.

The dog wags its tail and it whacks Dean in the leg. Dean then gets up and holds the shanty's door open.

In a commanding tone he says. "Toby get the fish and get on out of here!"

Springing into action, the dog secures the fish in his mouth. Carrying the fish Tobias trots out the door. Standing alongside one of the many ice fishing shanties scattered on the lake, two men point at the dog as it darts into the darkness.

Inside the shanty, breaking down fishing gear Dean thinks to himself; *Janis told me if she was the one who died first that she wouldn't want me to be alone. So, I'm going to try hard to show Kelly a good time tonight. She's so very sexy. Her gentle touch soothes me.*

He sighs and whispers, "Janis, I know, I promised."

Strapping on a backpack Dean then walks out of the shanty and into the windblown snow.

With the fish securely in his jaws, the dog hops through the deep snow and maneuvers up a bluff. Tobias then heads toward the blinking colored lights that decorate the old hunters' lodge.

At the backdoor of the lodge, Detective Sentieri hands Randy the caged kitten.

The detective says. "I'll see you later and you better save me a room."

Randy takes the cage into the pantry and takes the kitten out. Looking for food to feed the kitten Randy hears a scratching sound. He puts the kitten back in the cage and walks out of the pantry. Reaching the back porch, he opens the door and the dog proudly prances inside. With his sharp teeth clamped down on the fish the dog wags his tail.

Seeing the fish, Randy says, "Tobias what have you brought me?"

The dog puts the fish down at Randy's feet.

"Good boy." Randy says as he tosses a reward into the air.

"There you go Toby. The best smoked dear jerky in the county."

The dog snatches the treat out of the air and prances back outside.

With the fish in hand Randy goes back into the pantry.

He opens one of the swinging doors that separates the pantry from the bar area, and says. "Sweetheart, can you come here for a second?"

After she serves a customer some food and a drink she walks into the pantry.

Jennifer sees her husband cleaning the fish and says, "Should I put that aside for Dean?"

"Yes. He said that he's going to stop here some time tonight. But I don't know when." Randy replies.

"Is he bringing a Kelly Carlson with him?"

"I think so. Let's reserve the private dining room just in case." Randy then points towards the pantry. "Your bother in-law dropped the kitty off warning me to save a room for him."

"You can't pick your family." Jennifer replies.

Randy stops cleaning the fish to say, "You know everyone thinks that he gave me the money to open this place. I worked my ass off remodeling this place. When he starts paying for his room that's when he'll have a room. Otherwise he sleeps in the pantry."

"It's his birthday."

"I don't give a shit."

A terrifying scream is heard coming from the bar area.

The shriek sends chills down Jennifer's spine and she says, "What happened now?"

Randy puts down the fillet-knife and looks at her.

Again, from inside the bar area a patron is heard shouting "They found Tom's body and Vicky's been abducted! "

Jennifer hurries back through the swinging doors and finds everyone watching the television. Randy joins her and they all watch the news report. Everyone is horrified to learn that the cameraman's body was found, and that the news reporter is missing.

Living a dream

Wondering how she will escape, Martha crouches against the wall. In the distance she hears a door slam. Cringing in fear, she listens counting the approaching footsteps.

When the footsteps stop, she thinks; *Twelve steps to freedom.* Hearing the keys rattle against the steel door her heart thumps and she whispers, "God help me!"

Martha then hears the lock being turned and the door open. A pale-yellow light fills the doorway. She hides her face and remains silent. As if it makes her invisible, she holds her breath and closes her eyes tight. Hearing someone come into the room she remains still.

The moment seems to last for an eternity. Her muscles tighten. Terror stricken she presses her lips together. Feeling light headed Martha waits for the door to slam shut before she gasps for air. Hearing the door being locked she again counts the footsteps. Sitting in the darkness she is startled when she hears a moan

Responding, Martha gets to her feet. She franticly feels around in the darkness. She soon finds someone laying there. In her mind, Martha has been coping well with the situation. However, her body feels differently. She feels weak and dizzy. Grimacing, she clenches her stomach and falls to her knees. Hearing a moan again, she reaches out and feels someone who is bound and gagged. Exactly in the same manner she was.

Peeling the tape gingerly off her mouth Martha whispers, "Are you okay?"

A woman's drowsy voice replies, "Besides this headache, I'm fine."

Peeling the tape off the woman's wrist, Martha says, "My name is Martha. I'm so scared! My husband and I were attacked in the alleyway across the street from the diner. I think I'm getting sick."

Peeling the tape off her ankles the woman replies, "We'll be okay. Do you know where we are?"

Sitting back down, Martha says, "I think we're in a basement. Have you seen my husband, Gildardo?"

The disheveled woman replies, "No, I haven't." With her situation becoming evident Vicky grumbles, "Oh no. This can't be happening. Today was supposed to be one of the best days of my life."

Recognizing the voice, Martha hands Vicky a bottle of water. "Here have some." She then adds. "You're the news reporter, aren't you? Do you know what happen to my husband?"

Vicky's mind stops racing to consider; *How can I break the news to her. If I were her, I'd want to know.*

Vicky takes a small sip off the bottle, and answers, "Yes, he's dead Martha. I'm so sorry."

Martha begins sobbing.

Vicky reaches over and holds Martha. "The last thing I remember, I was loading equipment."

Vicky hears that Martha had stopped sobbing and so she hands the bottle back to her. "Thanks Martha, for the water. I was thirsty."

"You can thank our kidnapper he left them in a paper bag. I think there's food in the bag too, would you like me to check?"

"No thanks." Vick says as she thinks. *I wonder if the water was drugged.*

"Are you sure that my husband's dead?" Martha asks.

Sympathetically, Vicky replies, "Your husband was murdered. His body was found in the alleyway."

Martha again lets out a mournful cry.

Although she knows more details of the crime scene, Vicky does not go into detail.

Martha's eyes roll back as she crumbles to the ground. Vicky quickly helps her to sit up against the wall.

Despondently, Martha whispers, "I'm cursed!"

Holding the sobbing woman, Vicky says in a positive tone of voice, "Don't worry Martha we're going to find our way out of here. And, if you think your life's cursed, let me see, where should I start?" Vicky sighs and then continues to say, "I was an only child. My parents considered me extra baggage and were always too busy to care. When I was old enough, they sent me away to a boarding school. So, from an early age, I looked for love in the wrong places. I've been divorced twice. My first marriage ended when I realized that I liked his car better than him. I drove off in the car and left him at the gas station in New York. My second husband made me quit my job and move to his home town. And, when I caught him in bed with his ex, it broke my heart. I can't believe I wanted to have kids with that bastard."

Teary-eyed, Martha's stutters, "We were so perfectly happy. He loved our daughter so much."

Career case

At the Moon Lake Police Department law enforcement officers shuffle into a light green conference room.

Sanding over a table littered with crime scene photos, one detective whispers to himself, "This monster has to be caught."

Interrupting his train of thought several men and women walk into the room. They all take a seat at a long conference table. Another man carrying a briefcase also walks in the room. He opens his briefcase, takes out a stack of vanilla folders and passes them out. The Taskforce Commander, Jack Mahoney then walks into the room. The FBI Agents stand aside to let him walk by. Their eyes follow him while he makes his way to the front of the room.

From underneath his thick silver eyebrows, he scans over the attentive assembly.

In a calm voice, he says, "Unfortunately, we have discovered another victim."

On a large media screen, behind him is a family portrait of a man, his wife and child.

"Thomas J Cantrell, a cameraman, who worked for the local television news station. His body was found dismembered at the Moon Lake Cemetery. Preliminary autopsy reports confirm that a shoestring was used to strangle the victim. Also, Vicky Marcus, a local news reporter who was with Mr. Cantrell is believed to have been abducted by the perpetrators. Yes, because of the footprints in the snow. We now know there is more than one killer."

Hearing the news, the room is stifled. With help of a media screen and a laser pointer, Jack Mahoney uses related crime scene diagrams to illustrate facts. To provoke theories, he adds infamous serial killer's profile scenarios. Determined to apprehend the killer, the collection of homicide detectives listen attentively.

The Taskforce Commander then says, "As you can see preliminary forensic summaries of today's crime scene are consistent with the Shoestring Strangler's signature rituals. Crime scene technicians also recovered an autographed note claiming responsibility. The writing of the note and signature matches previous notes. DNA was extracted from this coded note and it has been sent to the lab. The latest note found at the cemetery crime scene also reveals that the killer plans to murder five more people by eight o'clock tonight."

A police officer sitting in the back of the room raises her hand. Jack Mahoney points at the officer and says, "You have a question?"

The woman stands and says, "Do you still believe that the perpetrators are residents of Moon Lake?"

Acknowledging the question, Jack nods his head, and states, "Yes, I do. And we expect to know more when we are finished processing the crime scene."

Jack Mahoney then holds up a folder, "Now let's get to work. Inside the case file you'll find the potential victims' profiles. The people targeted are residents of Moon Lake."

The officers open the folder and shuffle through the papers as the Taskforce Commander continues. He lists pertinent facts showing evidence to support that the killer's rage has escalated.

In a calm voice, Jack Mahoney states, "Today in broad daylight, in two different locations, these killers have dismembered their victims and abducted two females. One of the victims was dismembered less than one block from Norma Jean's Diner. With all these people walking around someone had to see something. I want every resident interviewed and every inch of this city searched!"

Moving on to include previous crimes scenes, the Taskforce Commander instructs the investigators to review the complete case file. Looking for clues, they begin to page through the documentation. The investigators pick apart every piece of evidence associated with the Shoestring Strangler slayings. Playing a theme song of a classic detective television series, a cell-phone's rings. A man dressed in a gray suit, wearing a burgundy tie, pulls out his cell-phone.

Turning off his cell-phone the red-faced man says apologetically, "Sorry about that."

Standing stoically behind the podium, the Taskforce Commander's icy stare gazes over the room. With this occurrence, the air in the room is stifling.

Wrapping up the briefing, Agent Mahoney says, "Listen up. The overkill at the crime scenes firmly suggest that theses slayings are personal." Jack Mahoney pauses for a moment then continues to say, "The killers threaten to murder five more people by eight o'clock. Tonight, we'll have surveillance teams at the Unicorn Theater, Hanson Manor and the Old Hunters' Lodge." With conviction in his eyes the Taskforce Commander then tries to sum up the meeting, "We're going to dragnet and put a pair of eyes on every street, alleyway and position drones in the sky. Let's keep communication between departments clear and concise. Let's solve this case before it becomes a career case."

Eager to do their job, the sound of papers shuffling fills the room as the taskforce dig into the files.

Learning on the fly

Hearing a scratching sound at the backdoor, Randy opens it. A gust of bone chilling wind accompanies the dog inside the lodge. Tobias shakes off the snow and then lies down.

Sitting at the bar a man shivers and says, "Dam Randy, did you have to open the door? And, I hope you didn't let that dog in here. You know, there's a law against animals in eating establishments."

Carrying a log to the large cobblestone fireplace, Randy smiles at his wife, and says, "Pour him one on the house."

The man thanks Randy and as he watches Jennifer mix the drink. When she is finished, she puts the glass on the bar. The man smiles and takes hold of it.

Twirling ice around with a straw, the man says, "I saw a picture of that dog in the newspaper. He was on someone's kitchen table eating their Thanksgiving dinner. An eye-witness said that he ate the whole turkey before launching himself through the widow. Jennifer, did you see that picture?"

Knowing that Tobias is harmless, Jennifer replies, "I've seen that picture. That wasn't Toby."

"Well, it sure looked like that dog to me."

Noticing that the conversation is bothering Jennifer, the man changes the subject. "I still can't believe how your husband fixed this old joint up."

Trying hard not to ignore him, Jennifer replies, "It's our little slice of paradise."

Putting his drink down the man goes on to say, "It wasn't long ago that Moon Lake was like a ghost town. Tourism was dead. Back then, this lodge had a reputation for being a sleazy bordello. Everyone called it, 'The Bedbug Hotel'. Yep, we we're going to burn this place to the ground." Thinking about a woman he had met years ago at the lodge the man sips off his drink. Wanting to reminisce aloud, he places the drink down on the countertop of the bar. However, before he can say anything a thumping sound is heard coming from upstairs.

Hearing the sound, Jennifer wipes her hands off and quickly goes up stairs. Chasing down the sound it leads her to room number seven. She quickly takes out her passkey and opens the door. Looking inside the room she is amused by what she sees. Zongzi is in a crouched position, hopping up and down on the bed. Realizing Zongzi's condition and that he acts out his dreams, she is not too surprised. Being careful not to wake him up, she creeps up closer.

Seeing him twitch his nose, trying not to burst out laughing, Jennifer places her hand over her mouth.

She then thinks; *Ah is he dreaming that he's a bunny? I hope Sandy's right. Maybe, Zongzi's paranormal dreams are connected to an outer sphere of reality. But, how could a dream reveal who the killer is?*

Seeing that Zongzi had stopped hopping, Jennifer waits for a minute before she becomes comfortable enough to leave the room.

Inside the dreamer's mind, Zongzi looks out through the rabbit's eyes. He watches along as the rabbit leaps and scampers along the fringe of the lake. Under a bright sun the rabbit stops and rests near the edge of the water. While it laps up the cool water, Zongzi can see the reflection of the black and white furry animal. Remaining silent, Zongzi feels the rabbit's rapid heartbeat.

Concentrating on his mission to find out the identity of the Shoestring Strangler, he looks for direction.

Zongzi can still hear Sandy's words, "Fill yourself with love. Be fluid, flexible and create attunement. Release anxieties from within. Become light as a feather."

What he also remembers is the passion behind her words. Instantly a cloud of disgust and hatred for the killer is dispersed from Zongzi's spirit. The oppressive pressure to find out who the killer vanishes. With his heart open vexing mental restraints untangle and a surreal sensation of bliss fills his mind. Along with the deep self-atonement he becomes confident. Self-assured, Zongzi breathes deep.

Sensing his transformation and appreciating his demeanor the rabbit stops hopping. The furry animal begins to nibble on a white rose.

In an instant, Zongzi is sitting in a patch of colorful wildflowers. He can hear chirping birds and crickets. A soft lake breeze fills him with whimsical notions of nonsense.

He rubs his eyes. "I've never seen sunshine so vivid. I feel so alive. I can hear the crickets keeping time while songbirds whistling from high. Wow. This must be love!"

Hearing a fluttering sound, he looks over to the lake and sees a swarm of butterflies.

Zongzi can hear their tiny voices sing, "With the new day's sun face the challenges, do not run. When the moment is here fill yourself with love and rise above the jeers. Use your gift to mend the rift. To end your plight, fill your mind with light. Become the thread that tightens the seam. To fulfill your purpose is our dream."

Before the dreamer can think of a reply the butterflies fly away. Their voices fade as they continue to sing. "Have faith in love that cannot be touched or seen. Rise above and find truth inside your dreams."

Zongzi smiles as he watches them flutter away.

From out of the corner of his eye he sees a shadow move in the water, "What is that? It looks like a giant sucker fish. It's as big as a bus!"

Stunned, Zongzi watches the shadow swims along the shoreline.

"It is a sucker fish."

The fish swims toword Zongzi.

"It's staring at me."

Within the fish's gaze, Zongzi feels his mind tingle. The chirp of the crickets and the whistles of the birds fade away. Pulled into a trance, his body goes limp and he falls to the ground.

"What's happening? I'm paralyzed!"

In the silence that follows, Zongzi feels his spirit being pulled out through his toes. When his vision comes back into focus, he is looking out through the fish's eyes. He sees the rays of sunlight that shine down into the water. Dumfounded, he gazes out and sees his body sprawled out on the lakeshore. Flabbergasted he wonders, "Inside this fish, how am I going to stop the killer? What am I going to do?"

Peering out through the fish's eyes he realizes that the fish is heading for deeper water.

Within his mind, Zongzi hears a tiny voice say, "It's nice to welcome you aboard today. My name is Cindy and I am here to help in any way. To reach your destiny in time, let serenity fill your mind."

Feeling his mind at ease, Zongzi replies, "Do you have the answers I need? Will you help me to stop the killer's bloody madness spree?"

"Yes, I am the vessel that will get you there before it is too late. I will assist you in ending this trail of hate. I will bring you to the one who knows the truth? To the reaper of fools and the one who collects debts long overdue? I understand your mission and I'm here to help you."

Zongzi tries to express the misery and sorrow that the killer left behind.

He says. "The pain the killer has caused may never end but the killer must not kill again."

Concentrating on getting to their destination, the fish is silent. Looking out through the eyes of the fish, Zongzi realizes that the deeper the fish swims, the darker it gets.

Cleanliness is Godliness

Inside a dimly lit room two dark figures use towels to wipe thick dark blood off their face and hands. After putting down the blood-soaked towels they walk across the room. Together they continue down a circular staircase. Moonlight shining through windows in the stairwell reveals the shadows of a woman and man. The man is tall and the woman, who is carrying a bag, has long hair. Reaching the bottom of the stairs they walk down a hallway.

The woman giggles and says, "Those so-called profilers. They know my next move by being a magnifying glass into my psyche? How do they come up with these harebrained ideas? They're no match for someone me. They're just plain silly."

Coming to the end of the hallway they go through a door and into a room. They walk across a concrete floor to a counter and sink.

The man sniffs the air, "I smell mildew? When we're finished, I want you to spray this room with bleach. Now let's get busy. Dump the bag."

Overturning the bag bloody surgical tools clink and clank against the stainless-steel surface.

"My babies." the woman says smugly.

One by one they begin the task of cleaning the bloodstained utensils in the sink. The man washes them in the sink. Using a washcloth, the woman wipes them off. She inspects them before she gently lays them on the counter.

Using a childlike tone of voice, the woman says. "Love and blood is what life is made of. The love that rained down from the sky was sowed with the blood that boiled up from below. Love and blood are what life is made of. You know I'm accustomed to cleaning up the mess. From an early age of nine, I found solace at staying busy. When my dad got pissed, he'd come home and knock everything off shelves. When he passed out, I swept up and put everything back in place. He treated mommy and me like garbage."

Relentless demonic voices overcome her thoughts. *Stick to the plan. The tools are now blessed and ready!*

Accustomed to theses intrusions within her mind, the woman looks at the man, "You and daddy look a lot alike. Remember what happen to him?"

The man smiles and nods his head yes.

The woman continues to say, "Okay, where should I begin? Let's see, my first tool was given to me on my twelfth birthday by you, my favorite uncle. When I unwrapped the present, I couldn't believe what I saw. A shiny lumberjack saw. I knew what you wanted me to do with it. And so, on that same day, I used it on my daddy. Honestly, it was hilarious. Remember? You tied my dad's hands behind his back but left his legs untied. Then, you threw a hangman's noose over a wood beam. You put the noose around daddy's neck and then pulled the rope until daddy was swinging in the air. Daddy churned his legs like he was riding a bicycle. Remember? His legs pumped slower and slower as his soul left his body. We laughed so hard my tummy ached. Then, you laid his body down on the table. Daddy's terrified bugged-out eyes were still wide open. When we saw this, we both started laughing again. Then, I got busy. I sawed as fast as I could until his arms and legs had plopped onto the floor."

With sinister gleams in their eyes they look at one another and giggle.

The woman then continues to say, "And, when it was over, we were both covered in blood. Remember what happen then? We both slipped and fell on the bloody floor. It was hilarious! I laughed so hard I pissed my pants." Admittedly she adds. "It was so sloppy compared to my latest masterpiece."

Using a washcloth, the man continues to scrub the suborn thick dark blood off their tools of madness.

Holding up a bloody knife the woman exclaims, "Our latest addition to the collection. Gets sharper with every slice." Handling the knife like it is priceless she wipes it off and sets it on the counter.

When they are finished, the woman undresses and goes into another room and takes a shower. Standing on the cold, brown and tan, mosaic tiled floor waiting for the water to run hot, the demented woman quivers. Feeling the water getting warmer, she puts her face into the stream of water. Steam begins to rise around the killer as she rubs a bar of soap in her hands. The hot shower begins to soothe the haunted mind and relaxes the killer's taut muscles. Basking in tranquility, the killer's eyes shine gleefully.

Slipping momentarily into a daze she surrenders to dementia. Inside her mind the concept of reality becomes stupendous. Adamant rationalizations ricochet between the ears as interjections of mayhem forges a pompous purpose.

Rinsing the soap off she sings. "Soon Moon Lake will be cleansed. Cleanliness is Godliness. And, Godliness is cleanliness."

Close by, in the adjoining room the man hears her singing. He smiles as he put the tools back in the bag.

Remembrance

Dusk begins to fall as Detective Sentieri drives past a snow-covered football field.

"Welcome to Moon Lake. There's the Northland Pines High School, wonder how the Eagles are doing?" Focusing he then says to himself. "It's time to solve the crime, grab the woman and get out of Dodge. Then we'll take a nice long vacation." Looking down the snowy street the Unicorn Theater comes into view. Hauntingly it reminds of the killings as the warm and fuzzy feelings of yesteryear disappear. To clear his mind, he turns on the radio.

After a commercial about vitamins that increase your testosterone, an announcer comes on and says, "Welcome back to Moon Lake Radio. Snow and wind are not stopping anyone from coming here. Moon Lake is flooded with tourist. Most are here to see the movie 'Shoestring Strangler'. Also, some are gearing up for the annual ice fishing contest or the snowmobile races. Now joining me on the phone is five-time winner of the snowmobile contest, Randy Sentieri. He is also is the proprietor of the Hunters' Lodge. Hey Rando Skidoo, I hear you're not competing in the race. Is this true and if it is why?"

"Maybe I should start taking those vitamins. But I just don't feel like it."

"I envy a man with few words. My listeners probably wish I was more like you. There's another reason we have you live here on Moon Lake Radio. Everyone's talking about the tonight's talent contest. Can you tell us more about it?"

"Yes, I can. Charlene, an accomplished singer is hosting tonight's talent contest. An array of contestants has entered. Singers, jugglers and a local ventriloquist will be performing beginning at nine tonight."

The announcer then says. "I hear that the winner of the contest will receive two tickets for a luxury cruise around the world. Is that correct?"

"That's right. And, right now on stage, contestants are already rehearsing. So, come on down to the Hunters' Lodge for some great entertainment, food and drinks."

Detective Sentieri reaches over and turns the radio off. Hearing his stomach rumble, he thinks; *Some of Ida's Swedish meatballs sure would hit the spot.*

Under gray clouds, snowflakes continue to drift aimlessly down as he pulls up to the theater. Getting out of the car, a chilling wind bites into his skin. He pulls his collar closer to his neck and walks toward the theater. Another man joins him walking across the street.

The man with a scarf around his face looks at Detective Sentieri and says, "Hey Rob, I knew you'd show up." The man then holds the door open and says, "Come on in, everyone's here."

The detective looks at the man and says, "Hey Ted. How's our Mayor doing today?"

"Busy as one-legged man in an as kicking contest. You know Mr. Sentieri, if you would have done your job ten years ago none of this would be happening."

Rob thinks; *Yea you were one of those who pressured your nephew into a confession. That closed the case and I got a direct order not investigate it any further.*

Without saying another word, they continue to walk into the theater and go different ways.

A cold sweat comes over the detective as he walks into the crowded theater. His cell-phone rings.

Recognizing the incoming number, he activates the call.

"Randy, tell me that saved me one of your bungalows."

In a regretful tone his brother replies, "We just heard it on the news and I want to let you know that Jennifer and I are both praying for you."

The detective stops in his tracks. "What's up?"

"Vicky's been abducted, and Tom's body was found dismembered at the cemetery."

"Tom? Have you seen Judy?"

"No. Everyone is at the Remembrance. Jennifer did tell me that Judy's still coming here after the movie to help out."

The detective pauses before he says. "Thanks for calling. I'll see you later."

The detective struggles to concentrate while he despondently hangs up the phone and thinks; *If anything happens to Vicky, I'm going to strangle someone.*

Inside the theater his mind relives the heinous moments of the past. Passing through the area of the bathrooms he remembers the bloody footprints that led into the women's bathroom. How he followed them to where they came from. He thinks back to when he walked into the theater. The first thing he saw was all the blood that was spattered across the theater's big white screen. The flashback becomes vivid and the rest of the ghastly scene comes into focus. Propped up in the front row seats the detective remembers seeing the limbless corpses. Walking toward the bodies he was careful not to disturb the crime scene. Along the way he had to step over dismembered body parts. Bloody arms and legs littered the isle of the theater. Finally reaching the victims he sees shoestrings neatly tied around each victim's neck. It was at this time when he heard a loud bang. Like a steel door being slammed.

It sounded like it came from under the stage. When I check that area, I didn't find anything.

Snapping out of the haunting memories the detective hears someone shout, "Rob over here!" He looks over to a group of people and sees Judy being consoled by friends.

Walking up to them he thinks the detective thinks; *It's starting all over again. When this monster slips up, I will be there. What's the motivation behind this? Whatever it is, it ends tonight.*

Being comforted by Ida and Sandy, in disbelief Judy's blank, glassy eyed, gaze says it all.

"Tommy's dead."

Wringing her hands, she panics.

"The killer has Vicky and the police have arrested Richard and Lexis. They think that they're the killers."

Everyone is visibly shaken and the surreal moment is hard to swallow. All at once, everyone tries to get a word in.

In the commotion Ida's husband pulls the detective aside and says, I think you should get down there to help Lexis and Richard. Lexis couldn't be involved with the killings. She can't stand the sight of blood. She almost passed out when I took her to get a flu shot. You know that we took care of her while Dean was in prison. I've grown to love Lexis. I can't lose her too." Lloyd then takes out a handkerchief and wipes away the tears from his face. "Please Rob get down there."

The group of devastated friends all look at the detective.

The detective then says, "If they're innocent they have nothing to worry about. The police are under a lot of pressure to catch the killers and they're going to follow every lead. No matter how farfetched it is." The detective then raises his hand. "I want everyone to calm down. I'm going down there right now. Nothing's going to happen to Lexis or Richard."

Hearing this, Judy's wipes tears from her eyes. Remembering how Dean was railroaded, she pictures her husband being slammed around by interrogators. Fearing for his life Judy thinks. *Richard carries a knife and he'll use it.*

Terrified to the core Ida hands the detective's a bag and says. "Here's some food. Please make sure that Lexis is okay. She's like a daughter to me."

With a reassuring look the detective replies, "Everyone is going to be okay. When I find out anything I will call."

Putting his arms around Judy and his wife, Lloyd says, "We've got a première to get ready for."

Ida looks at him and nods her head. "Lloyd, that's a good Idea. Is that okay with you Judy?"

"How will I able to do anything knowing my brother has been murdered? I am so screwed up." Judy then turns to the detective and says, "Rob will you please make sure Richard and Lexis make it back in time. They did a lot of work getting the theater ready."

After Judy, Ida and Lloyd walk away Sandy says, "Detective can I catch a ride with you to the station? I need to report something that I saw during the Remembrance Ceremony."

Feeling a sharp pain in his chest the detective strains to focus. "Let's go, the car is across the street."

Noticing his discomfort Sandy says, "Are you okay?"

Rubbing his arm, the detective says, "I'll feel better after I eat something."

Guiding light

Leaving the warmth of the theater, Sandy and Detective Sentieri walk into the windblown snow.

Again, feeling the sharp pain in his chest, the detective thinks; *I'm on my way Vicky.*

Soon as they are both get inside the car the detective starts the engine.

While the engine warms up the detective turns to Sandy and says, "Lexis mentioned that you make a special type of wine. A wine that can help your subconscious to connect with the Universal Cloud. What is the Universal Cloud?"

In a calming voice Sandy replies, "The Universal Cloud connects everything there ever was or will be. It is a higher perspective that has no limitations or boundaries. Since the beginning, human kind has been developing an inner compass that will lead us to the Universal Cloud. We are driven by a deep inner urge to reestablish this connection. Zongzi's trying to learn how to harness his inner urges as we speak. One of the first things he must do is to walk away from himself and earthly desires. If successful, his subconscious will be accepted into the realm of spiritual enlightenment."

Flicking a toggle switch the detective turns on the windshield-wipers and puts the car in gear.

Driving down the snowy street he then says, "So, your homemade wine will put Zongzi into a dreamscape where he'll find out who the killers are. Do you really believe this will work?"

"Yes. With simple ingredients the natural soothing effects of the wine are enhanced. This enrichment will allow Zongzi to be more aware. Within the dreamscape anything is possible. And in this higher plane of reality he'll be able to find out who's responsible for the killings."

With the engine warm the detective turns the window defroster on high, "When he wakes up, he'll know who is responsible for the strangulations?" he asks.

"Yes, Zongzi will know the identity of the Shoestring Strangler."

Thinking about what Sandy said, the detective tries to surmise. "The wine allows Zongzi, in a dreamscape to see the truth."

"Yes, his objective is to flow within the All-Knowing universal stream of consciousness."

"I can see in some respects. But, using wine to induce this deep sleep makes it dangerous."

"Zongzi and I, both realize the potential danger. We believe that it's worth the risk." Sandy replies.

While the wiper swipes snowflakes back and forth off the windshield, intrigued, the detective then says. "So, the gist of his journey is for Zongzi to be adaptable?"

"Yes, to leave himself behind and be immersed in the flowing essence of love."

"Is he experiencing this dreamscape now?"

"Yes, he's at the lodge, up in his room in a deep sleep. When Zongzi is flowing through dreamscapes he will be absorbed into his surroundings. When this transformation is complete, he becomes a viable extension of the truth."

Trying to understand the detective says, "What happens when he discovers who the killer is?"

"This is where things get fuzzy. Zongzi will have to be able to wake himself up. If he doesn't, he will be pulled into many more dreamscapes. Experiencing these will dilute any vision of the identity of the killer."

Taking his eyes off the road, the detective opens the paper bag Ida had given him. He takes out a meatball and eats it and his stomach growls for more.

He eats another one and looks at Sandy. "Why do you need to go to the station? What did you see at the Ceremony?"

"I saw a little black splotch dash inside the theater."

"What's a back splotch and why is it so important to tell the police?"

"A splotch is a lost and frightened soul. It's a piece of darkness that takes refuge inside the unsuspecting. These cantankerous parasites prey on sick minds."

"So, Sandy, are you saying that the killer was at the remembrance?"

"I believe so. I could feel a toxic aura festering inside the theater. But the reason I ask to go with you is to tell you about what Zongzi is going to do."

After eating another meatball, the detective says, "Sandy, can I ask you some more questions?"

"Ask away."

"Are you absolutely sure that Lexis and Richard have nothing to do with the Shoestring Strangler's atrocities? Are they as harmless as they seem?"

"I believe so. And Detective I have seen Lexis's palm. The lines are crystal clear. She is like rain. A God sent. The killer or killers are egotistical psychopathic monsters."

Getting closer to the police station the detective thinks to himself; *If Sandy's alternative investigative insights can help, I'm all for it.* Interested in her insights the detective says, "Sandy, can you tell me more about reading palms?"

"An endeavor of love engraves them. Like a record all the answers of our journey are imbedded deep in the lines. I'm talking about the lines in your palm. They are poured out by the pith of the soul. We are defined by these lines. By the winds of change theses lines are etched, honed and polished to perfection. Ones that run straight or fork out are the roads drawn by destiny. Follow them like a map and you will see your destination. All the answers are right there in the palm of your hand." Sandy replies.

Her voice is relaxing, and the conversation calms the Detective's mind and he says, "You have a very calming way about you. Were you born a fortuneteller?"

She replies, "It is a gift and takes time to develop ways to recognize signals of how the person is in at that moment. The most apparent ways are by reading faces and body language. Look beneath the surface and you will discover their intentions. Tune in to what's behind the words, their actions and choices to reveal their future. See the truth by looking deep into their eyes. You'll see it reflect outward from their soul. Study current intentions simply by recognizing posture and facial expressions." Seeing that the detective is very interested Sandy continues, "Palm lines reveals the deep underlining substance of a person. Other features may reveal what is on the surface. Like your studies in law enforcement that teach you about interviewing. To observe body language, folding arms or fidgeting can give insights. Other distinguishing traits of the head, feet and face also can give insight into the mind. Still, another way is by touch. A sincere touch unveils the inner-truth within their soul. But, the most powerful way to gain insight is to follow our internal guiding light. When harnessed, gut feelings give you direct connection to the universal cloud." Sandy pauses for a moment and then says, "Detective, the ability to traverse trails of past residue of someone you must use the compass that exists deep within your being."

The detective nods his head agreeably and replies, "Yes. Gut feelings have paid off quite often."

Driving down the snowy road Sandy says, "When we're done at the station can we check in on Zongzi?"

The detective looks at her and nods his head.

Breakout

Sitting in the pitch-black darkness Martha whispers, "I can't stop shivering."

Vicky puts her arm around her and says, "We are going to get out of here."

Taking quick, short breaths, the distraught woman replies, "I'm not feeling good. I'm dizzy and I'm cramping."

Vicky says, "This guy's the type that gets his kicks from total dominance over his victims. I also heard that the killer also believes that he's doing God's will by weeding out the bad apples."

Interrupting their conversation, rattling keys are heard coming down the stairway.

Listening to the approaching footsteps Vicky whispers, "I'm going to get his attention and you run."

Sensing the maniacal aura that precedes the abductor, Martha's heart races and eyes grow wide. Hearing the door swing open, Martha and Vicky watch the dark figure walk into the room. Too dark to see his face, they can see the outline of a large man.

Ready to execute a furious attack, Vicky clenches her fists. Determined to help Martha, she charges at the man and shrieks, "You bastard!"

The two begin to struggle in the darkness. The man then puts his hand over Vicky's mouth and she bites into the man's thumb.

Hearing the man moan Martha darts through the door. Not looking back, she runs up the stairs and pushes open a door. She sees the lake and with no coat or hat she runs into the windblown snow. Underneath the moon lit sky, she recognizes the multicolored blinking lights that line the roof of the old hunters' lodge. She continues to run down an icy slope toward the lodge. She then loses her footing, slides down the hill and onto the ice-covered lake.

With moonlight shining through the doorway Vicky fights relentlessly. She knees the man in the groin.

The man buckles over and moans. "You bitch. You're going to pay for that."

Vicky darts towards the door. The man reaches out and viciously pulls her back by her hair. He throws Vicky back into the dark room. Repressing his pain, the angry man blocks the doorway. Trying again to get through the doorway Vicky screams and charges toward the man. The man backhands her across the face. The force spins her body around and her eyes lose focus. Vicky's body goes limp and falls to the ground. The man then walks up the stairs, out the door and locks the door behind him. Holding his groin, he follows the fresh footprints in the snow.

Back on her feet, Martha runs into the blowing snow. She runs out to the center of the lake and looks along the shoreline. She again spots the lodge. Martha's runs towards the lodge as fast as she can. The adrenalin rush overrides the freezing wind biting into her face. Still feeling dizzy she stumbles trying to maintain her stride toward the lights.

Grimacing in pain the man gingerly makes it down the slope and onto the lake. Following footsteps in the snow the man continues after Martha.

Not far ahead Martha slips again and falls. Her chin hits the frozen lake and a sharp pain accompanies a flash of light. Unconscious her mind drifts off. Through the fog in her mind Martha watches as Gildardo plays peek-a-boo with their daughter.

Front desk

At the police station, reporters jockey for position.

Flipping over another page in his notebook a news reporter with a British accent says. "Agent Mahoney, can you tell us anything more about the latest victims of the Shoestring Strangler."

"Yes, victim grew up in the same neighborhood that the other victims did. And like previous slayings, head, torso were left intact and a shoestring tied in a bow around the neck." the Taskforce Commander replies.

The reporter jots down in his notebook and says, "So, crime scene rituals were consistent?"

"Yes, the killer dismembered the body in the same manner. And, like the victim in Chicago an autographed note was retrieved from the victim's mouth. The note said that five more people will be murdered by eight o'clock." The Taskforce Commander then waves off taking any more questions and says, "I'll schedule another briefing later on today."

A young woman stylishly dressed for a warmer climate then shouts. "Agent Mahoney!"

However, she fails to get the attention of the speaker as he continues to walk out of the room.

She rings the silver service bell on the counter and blurts, "I've learned that two suspects have been taken into custody. Can you confirm this and tell me who these suspects are?"

Making his way through the reporters the Taskforce Commander does not answer.

The woman continues to ring the bell. "Can I get some answers over here?"

Sitting behind a cluttered desk a frustrated woman looks up at her. "Weren't you standing over there when Agent Mahoney held his news conference?"

The woman snidely replies. "Yes, I was."

"Then you should remember when the detective told you reporters to let us do our job. Can't you see how busy we are?"

Overhearing what the woman asked, reporters clamor around the desk and continue to ask the police officer for any information about the two possible suspects.

Fuming, the police officer sighs displeasingly and picks up the phone. "Can you send someone down here? These bloodhounds are suffocating me!"

The voice on the phone replies. "All available officers are out on the streets." Like a warning shot the red-faced woman slams the phone down. Instantly, the room is quiet as the police officer stands up and snarls at them.

Interrogation

On the second floor of the police station. Lexis sits inside a small room. She cringes when a detective slides his chair closer to her.

The detective whispers in her ear. "Remember the night we went to our high school prom? You look so hot in that red dress. We danced and drank that spiked punch. You told everyone that we were going to be married. Remember what happen when I got you home? Yea, you told me that your parents were gone for the night. You pulled me upstairs into your room and said that you wanted 'to do it'."

With tears beginning to roll down her cheeks Lexis replies, "I don't remember. And the next time I saw you at school, you ignored me. You never even said one word to me after that night."

"You know why? We had sex and when we were done you grabbed your doll and sat in the corner talking to it. You said that you were going to kill me and chop me into little pieces. Remember that?"

"I don't remember having sex with you! And you spread all those rumors about me at school. I lost all my friends. Why did you do that to me? You said that you loved me."

"How could anyone love someone as whacked out as you? The fantasy is over slut! We've read your diary. We know about your sick plan to kill Ida and Lloyd. You hated them for having you sleep in your dead sister's room. We also know that your accomplice and you left the remembrance service together. We have an eyewitness that puts Richard and you at the cemetery." The detective leans back in his chair and adds, "Oh yea, we've talked to your real mother. You remember Molly? She said when you were a little girl that you loved to help her to chop people up. She told us that you would sing while cleaning up the mess. Your mother said that you're sick in head."

Feeling light headed, Lexis thinks. *Why are you bringing up all these things? I don't remember?* Looking straight into the interrogator's eyes Lexis shouts, "Tommy was my friend. I grew up with him. I didn't kill him!"

The interrogator looks into the mirror on the wall and shakes his head displeasingly.

Watching from the other side of the two-way mirror Jack reads an email from the DNA Ancestry testing facility:

Resourcing the Federal DNA database, birth records and genealogies we can use the crime scene DNA to confirm lineage. Using the family tree and line of descent we will be able to determine the identity of the Shoestring Strangler. Expect an email from us very soon.

Looking at the clock on the wall, the Taskforce Commander whispers, "Five-forty-three, times running out."

Grimacing he washes down a pair of aspirin with a glass of water. Listening to Lexis and watching her body language he thinks; *She continues to show empathy in her actions and words. The profile does not fit. Maybe when we question the gravedigger, we'll get a different reaction. The only reason I see that she is a suspect is that her DNA links her to the killer. I wonder if Dean even knows that he's related to his adopted daughter.*

Hearing someone pounding on the door Jack stands up. When the door swings open, he sees that Dean Stein is being held back by two detectives.

Dean yells out. "What the hell's going on here? Why is that bastard alone with my daughter! That the son-of-a-bitch raped her!"

Struggling to break free Dean elbows the officer in the gut. Breaking free from their grasp he pushes his way into the interrogation room. With stretched out hands he lunges at the interrogator. Two detectives converge on Dean and force him to the ground.

Squeezing his words through the choke hold, Deans gurgles. "Lexis!"

Understanding the fury in Dean's eyes, Jack says. "Hold him until he calms down and then cut them both loose."

Mentally drained Dean's body goes limp. When he pulls himself together, he is permitted to go into the interview room.

Seeing her stepfather come through the door. Lexis shouts. "Papa! Get me out of here!"

Walking down the hallway Jack thinks; *If this next interview ends up like the last, we're going to be right back where we started.*

Jack then goes back into the observation room to watch over the next interrogation.

A detective who is sitting at a steel table across from the suspect says, "So, Rich, remember how we caught you using your bow and arrow to catch fish? Remember what I told you back then? That I'd put you in jail one day. Since then, I have I've seen you do some strange things. I've seen your passion to kill. Seen you kill possums, squirrels and rabbits for no reason except to get your kicks. Last spring didn't I catch you kill a dear out of season? You know that you're still on probation for that."

Folding his arms Richard leans forward over the table and calmly says. "Why am I down here? "

The interrogator replies, "It's because of your sick obsession. You get a trill when you kill. No matter how big or small. You get your kicks from killing bees, drowning earwigs and even stamping on ants? I've seen the contraptions you've built to catch them. I've known you my whole life. You get a rush from squishing and exterminating life. The first time I met you was when you were walking down the street stepping on June-bugs. You were laughing saying. 'I can hear and feel them crunch when I step on them.' Remember what you did in the third grade? I do. A mouse ran across the floor and you jumped up and stomped on it in front of the whole class. Is this why you call yourself the exterminator? Yep, you're a real weirdo. A lowlife loser whose sick obsession is to kill." The detective then gets up, walks over by the suspect and gets face to face and whispers. "Come on Rich, you know Lexis's spilling her guts out in the next room. She saying you did it all."

The officer returns to sit at the table across from the suspect. He folds his arms and leans back in his chair. The officer gives the suspect a smirk, nods his head and smiles.

Richard puts his arms on the table, leans forward and says. "You're a spoiled piece of shit. That is why you became a cop. So, you could carry handcuffs and arrest people. You are a dumb-shit with a badge that needs his ass kicked."

The detective leans forward, puts his hands on the table and glares into the suspects eyes, "Did you just threaten me?"

Rich replies, "No. You ain't worth it. But what comes around goes around, wimp."

"Rich, want to know what I'm waiting for? I'm waiting for you to go for your knife. Because, that will be the last thing you ever do. I promise!"

Richard leans forward, puts his head in his hands and sighs. Another detective walks into the room and says, "Come on Mr. Grayson. Looks like you're carrying the whole world on your back. Come clean and tell the truth. You will feel better."

The suspect fidgets in his chair and shouts. "I did not kill Janis! She was Judy's best friend."

The police officer shouts back. "Are you getting mad? We have DNA proof that you are the Shoestring Strangler and that you killed them all."

Richard tries to calm himself, he takes a deep breath and leans back in the chair. "I don't know what you're waiting for. I'm not going to confess to something I didn't do!"

"Why are you getting mad at us? We're just doing our job." the interrogator sitting across from Rich says.

Trying to coax the suspect into a confession, the other detective puts his hand on suspect's shoulder and says calmly, "Your neighbors think you're sick in the head. They've told me that you like to mutilate animals. That you bury squirrels alive up to their heads. Then run them over with the lawnmower. Come on Richard you're a very sick individual. Let it out and you'll feel better."

"I never did that. And why would I kill all those people!"

The detective sitting across from the suspect then says, "Because you believe that the victims had made a deal with the devil. Maybe you believe that God told you to do it. To save them from fiery pits of hell."

Richard looks up and glares. "You've been in my pocket ever since Jeff was murdered in Chicago!"

"This isn't about him. Richard, this is about you coming clean." the detective says and leans back in his chair.

The suspect then looks into the two-way mirror and says, "Are you as dumb as these two sons-of-bitches."

In the observation room, the Task Force Commander puts away his phone. He uses both hands to wipe the tension off his face. The Taskforce Commander then let out a deep sigh and shakes his head slowly side to side.

He pushes a button that activates the intercom speaker inside the interview room," Okay guys, I've seen enough. Cut him loose."

The two detectives look into the mirror in disbelief. The detective who was sitting down joins the Taskforce Commander in the observation room.

The detective throws his hands out. "What about the DNA. The hair follicles and fingernails that were recovered at the crime scenes?"

Agent Mahoney looks him in the eye, "A call just came in from surveillance. A drone captured their whereabouts at the time of the murders. So, I want you to cut them both loose. Have a squad escort them back to the theater. But don't let them out of your sight. Their lives are in danger."

In another room of the police station, Sandy and Detective Sentieri look at a wall covered with pictures.

Pointing at diagrams related to the case, Detective Sentieri says, "Crime scenes are blatant, executed with perverse passion and precision."

Sandy says, "Until the killer is caught Moon Lake's residents are not safe."

The door opens and they both turn around to see the Task Force Commander walk into the room.

The Taskforce Commander walks up to Sandy and the detective.

Reaching out to shake the detective's hand, he says, "Rob, can you give me any insight on this mystery?"

"Speaking of insight Jack, this is Sandy Adams. She's widening the scope of investigating possibilities by harnessing the subconscious by using dreamscapes. She also believes that the killer was present at the Remembrance Ceremony."

Agent Mahoney shakes Sandy's hand, "Miss Adams, welcome to the team. We can use all the help we can get. And, I agree with her that the killer or killers were in attendance. We do have agents watching live feeds from the theater. There are cameras all over the building, including the basement. While we were installing them, we have discovered a metal hatch in a room beneath the stage. We found it under stage props and junk. It is an old access tunnel that goes down into the sewer system."

The detective says, "When I first walked into the crime scene ten years ago. I heard a metal door slam."

Looking at the Taskforce Commander, Sandy says, "Are Lexis and Richard suspects?"

"Two people fitting their descriptions were seen leaving the cemetery in the van owned by the television station. But they are no longer suspects. While they were being interrogated, I got a call from the Video Surveillance Team. They verified Lexis and Rich's whereabouts at the time of the murders."

Lexis then says. "Are there any suspects?"

"No suspects, no leads." the Taskforce Commander replies. Pointing to the wall he then says, "The staging of the crime scene was different from the rest. The blood of latest victim was splattered on the gravestones of the previous victims. Is that a ritual to unite all the victims? I don't know. All I know is that when this is over, I'm throwing my phone in the lake and going to retire."

Fishing for clues, together they study and compare crimes scene data.

Pointing out the latest forensic reports, Agent Mahoney says, "We believe the DNA recovered from the eyeball down in Chicago originates from the killer. Hair follicles recovered at the recent crime scenes are bogus. Our technicians believe that they were planted by the perpetrators."

Detective Sentieri slowly moves his head side to side in disbelief, "The complexity of crime scenes baffles me. The perpetrators still take their time to leave evidence and a neatly tied shoestring."

Wondering aloud, Sandy says, "Shoestrings are tied to unite the shoelace. And splashing blood on the graves is a symbol of unification."

Task Force Commander then says, "That's sound logical. The only thing I want to figure out is how to catch them before they kill again. Profilers do agree that the killer or killers are stalking the victims. And that local residents are the target."

Detective Sentieri says, "Thanks, Jack, for helping us to sift through the facts. We're going to be heading down to the lodge."

The Task Force Commander walks them down the corridor to the door and says, "It was nice to meet you Miss Adams. Rob, check in with me later.

Before the Taskforce Commander walks away, he says, "The killer said five more will be murdered by eight o'clock tonight. So, we don't have much time to figure this out. So, if Martha and Vicky are two of the five, there is three more people being targeted. And Rob you are from the targeted neighborhood."

Fiddle Fish

Like a kite riding the breeze, the tide carries the suckerfish along with Zongzi's spirit into deeper water. Looking out through the fishes' eyes, Zongzi imagines; *I could get used to being a fish. Wow, over there's a school of minnows. They swim together in such a tight formation. It reminds me of those old warplanes at the air show.* With this thought his brain is whitewashed and goes blank. He ponders; *Where am I? I have gills and scales? Am I a fish?* Realizing that his mind is fading back and forth he then thinks; *I'm losing my grip. Sandy warned me, the clock's ticking. Wait a minute, think about the victims of the Shoestring Strangler. I must focus!*

Hearing Zongzi thoughts and sensing his frustrations, the fish's tail pushes steadily side to side through the cool lake waters. Using the mind to communicate, the fish thinks. *To say what's on your mind. Say it in a rhyme. Strain to regain the train of thought. It's all we got.*

The challenge to speak in rhymes challenges Zongzi's mind. He realizes how it does help him to concentrate on what he has to say. So, he thinks before he reveals his thoughts; *Who is the one that I need to see. The one who will reveal the truth to me?*

By way of thought, the fish quickly answers; *If anyone can grant your wish it would be the Speckled Fiddle Fish.*

Zongzi then thinks; *Can you tell me more about this Speckled Fiddle Fish? The one who can grant me my desperate wish?*

Confident in thought, the suckerfish replies; *My name is Jalopy. And, it's my mission to get you where you need to be. To bring you to the one you need to see. We are on a steady pace and on our way to a very secrete place. To meet with an amazing fish who will grant you your wish. She inspires all of us to be at our best. Not to wallow in self-pity or to regret. To face life's challenges, to pass life's test. When life takes its' toll and the hoop snakes are on a roll. When it comes down to push and shove, the Speckled Fiddle Fish inspires us all to rise above. To take the high road, the path that leads to love.*
Feeling inspired, the fish continues to think; *Look ahead, there's the circle of stones that rest on ancient bones. They also mark the doorway to worlds unknown. A place to gather on mid-summer's eve. To join in the dance of merriment that sets the spirit free.*
Looking ahead near the bottom of the lake, Zongzi sees large blue stones aligned in a circle. Inside the circle he also sees a collection of fish.
Amazed Zongzi thinks. *Look at all the different kinds of fish. This is the place to receive a wish. There's muskellunge swimming in a line with northern pike following close behind.*
As the suckerfish swims closer they also see a line of largemouth bass swimming in a circle. Zongzi watches as they swim around a school of bluegills. In the center of all the activity is a large spotted fish. Like a sidekick there is also a minnow swimming next to the prehistoric looking spotted fish.
The suckerfish thinks boastfully; *Look ahead, there's the one who will grant your wish. The Grandmaster of ceremonies the Speckled Fiddle-Fish.*
Trying to concentrate as hard as he can, Zongzi sends his thoughts to the Speckled Fiddle Fish; *Time is running out and I need to know without a doubt. Please reveal the truth to me. To know the Shoestring Strangler's identity. Please listen to this desperate plea.*
With reverence to oratory, a thought bellows throughout Zongzi's mind; *The loss of innocent lives, we all can hear their mournful cries. The killer spreads misery as far as the eye can see. We can feel the victim's sadness and grief. The same goal we do share. That justice for all is swift, relentless and fair.*

Zongzi quickly replies; *There's no time to waste. Innocent lives are at stake. Tell me the killer's identity before it's too late.* The fiddle-fish swims closer and looks deep into the eyes of the suckerfish; *Step in tune to understand what you feel. Allow the inner truth to release goodwill. Lose yourself, let love for others fill your sail. To see all things, tune in the spirit and you will never fail.*

With a gaze of bedazzlement, the suckerfish thinks quietly; *Heed the Speckled Fiddle Fish, fly far and fast. Keep your eyes forward. Do not dwell on the past.* From out of the corner of the eye the suckerfish sees movement and thinks; *Is that a tasty frog?*

The suckerfish quickly snaps its head to the side. The fish bites down and takes the bait. Instantly the metal hook digs into the side of the fish's mouth. The suckerfish's head moves side to side trying desperately to break free.

Zongzi can feel the fish's pain and distress. The hook yanks the fish up and out of the water. The retching pain of the hook tugging at the fish's mouth is agonizing. The fishing line then pulls the fish up out of the water.

Through the fish's eyes Zongzi can see the fish being lifted up over the lake. He also sees that they are being pulled up toward green and blue flashing lights. Zongzi watches in amazement as they rise high above the lake. The blinding lights shatters Zongzi's mind. Trying to comprehend what he sees his jaw drops wide open in awe.

Ready or not

While walking by room number seven Jennifer hears a thump. Remembering that Sandy told her to check on Zongzi, she quickly takes out her passkey and opens the door. She then quickly walks in to find him sleeping soundly.

Listening to him snore, she thinks; *The dream-detective is on a stake out or maybe I should say a dream-in.* She then is startled when Zongzi sits up and opens his eyes. She moves closer and sees that his eyes are shaking side to side.

With an inquisitive look on her face Jennifer whispers, "Are you okay?"

Zongzi leans his head back and opens his mouth. His face grimaces in pain. Tears begin to flow from his eyes. Careful not to wake him up she quickly leaves the room. Locking the door behind her she runs downstairs.

Walking toword the bar she makes a phone call. "Sandy something's going wrong. Zongzi's in a lot of pain."

"I'm on my way." Sandy replies.

A group of patrons stand up from the table and walk to the foyer.

Jennifer walks up to their table, "Thanks for stopping by."

Putting on their coats one of them says, "We'll be back after the movie."

Jennifer then clears a table off and carries the dishes behind the bar. After wiping off the table she puts a basket of fish into the fryer.

Her husband then walks in the room and joins other patrons sitting at the bar.

Looking at the television Randy says. "Look, we're on TV."

Hearing this Jennifer comes around the bar and sits down beside him.

On television a news reporter says. "In 1881, the three-story lodge was constructed on the shoreline of Moon Lake by a wild game hunter. The lodge and its seven bungalows were built using only timber logs and wooden nails. In the early twenties the lodge also served as the general store and post office. The property went through several owners before Randal Jon, Sentieri purchased and refurbished this rustic hideaway. Tonight, broadcasting live from the old hunters' lodge is Charlene Summers. She is an accomplished singer and family research specialist. Her talent show is simply the best. Tonight, contestants will be competing to join Charlene's talent show aboard the Aphrodite. Yes, the winner of the talent show will win two tickets to sail around the world. The two-hundred-forty-day journey departs from the Port of New York on New Year's Eve Day."

A man standing by the stage says to Charlene. "Do you really think Lexis has a chance?"

"She's a frontrunner that's for sure."

The man puts on his coat and then says. "I got to get to the theater. They want us ushers to show up early. So, I've got to get going. I will be back after the movie. What time does the show start and you are going to sing some songs, right?"

Charlene replies. "I going to give enough time for everyone to get here after the movie lets out. And yes, I will be singing before and after the contest."

The man gives Charlene two thumbs up and heads for the door.

A woman sitting at the bar puts down a steaming cup of coco and says, "I wonder if all this snow will keep people from going to the movie. Besides, the ticket prices are way too high. On an auction website, a pair of balcony seats sold for fourteen-hundred dollars. Instead of paying that kind of money, I rather just stay here and get a good seat for the contest."

Sitting in a reserved section of the Unicorn Theater Judy, Ida and Lloyd listen as a voice is heard over the speakers. "All ushers please report to the lobby."

Looking at the empty theater seats in their section, Judy wonders out loud, "Looks like Richard and Lexis are going to miss the movie. They worked really hard for this. What a bummer." After a slight pause Judy then says, "Lexis's going to miss the contest too. She was looking forward to being on television. What do you think is happening to them down at the station?"

Ida replies, "I don't know. It feels like everything is going downhill. I just hope that the movie gives us some closure."

Lloyd puts his arm around his wife and says, "We'll all get through it together, whatever happens."

Ida looks at her husband and smiles.

Lloyd takes hold of Ida's hand and says, "And don't worry dear I'm cleaning Shannon's room out tomorrow."

Ida kisses her husband on the cheek and says, "I love you Lloyd."

Ushers begin to shuffle in people as the theater quickly fills up. Then a violin is heard while words scroll across the screen; *"My soul aches because I long for your touch. To hear your laughter, see your smile I love so much. Our footsteps of the past were left side by side. It is so hard to smile without you in my life. There's no one to hold so I walk alone. Nowhere to go because without you there's no home. A simple fact that's true. I will try to move on. But I will never forget you." This heartfelt poem was written by Dean Stein in memory of his wife, Janis.*

Outside the theater a police squad pulls up with emergency lights flashing. A long black limousine pulls up behind the police car. A chauffer gets out of the car and opens the backdoor. Dean, a woman, Lexis and Richard get out and walk up the steps of the theater.

Inside the theater Lexis takes Dean by the arm and looks at his date. "Kelly are you and Papa going to the talent show?"

The woman replies. "We wouldn't miss it for the world."

Walking alongside of Lexis, Richard adds. "Let's just hope the killer is caught."

Seeing them walk in an usher quickly escorts them to their seats.

Who's next?

Walking out of a thick fog Vicky sees a crowd of people. The closer she gets her heart feels lighter and lighter. Hearing a familiar voice anticipation fills her mind.

"Welcome home we've been waiting for you."

With joy exploding from her heart Vicky cries out. "Is that you? Amy, is that you?"

"Yes, it's your sister." Stepping out of the bright sunlight the young woman hugs Vicky. "We've been watching over you and I am so proud of what you've done with your life."

Vicky's emotions shine through her eyes. "You're beautiful! I haven't seen you since you were in the hospital. You had lost all your hair and were in so much pain. Now look at you! This is the way I remember you with long flowing hair." Vicky looks deep into her sister's eyes. "Your courage inspired me, I thought about you every day."

"I never left you. I saw how my death changed you. It helped you to become who you are. And I love you for being so strong. We are blessed to be able to share this moment face to face. There are some others here who would like to give you a hug."

Vicky's eyes widen seeing other family members and friends crowd around her, "Is this heaven?"

Sandy and Detective Sentieri walk outside into the windblown snow. They both hurry to the car with the freezing wind biting into their skin. Once inside the car they strap on seatbelts and the detective starts the engine. The engine hums as the detective allows it to warm up.

Wanting to distract himself from the investigation the detective says. "Any plans for the holidays?"

"Actually, Zongzi and I have been saving up to take a vacation."

"So, the two of you are in a relationship?"

"Not romantically. We grew up together. The last few months have been full of ups and downs for both of us. We would like to just get away and concentrate on our music."

"Oh, you're musicians."

"Yes. I play guitar and Zongzi plays harmonica."

Sandy then thinks to herself; *Zongzi has put his life on the line again for me. If I think about it too much I won't feel right. And these selfish thoughts will distract from helping others. God please guide Zongzi and me. I don't deserve any favors from You. I have been very selfish. I know that I can be a better person. I do love You and thank You for all Your blessings.*

The car heater slowly begins to warm the inside of the car. Detective Sentieri puts the car in gear and they begin to drive down the street.

"Is it okay if I turn the radio on?" Sandy asks.

The detective responds by nodding his head.

Sandy turns the radio on. The song playing has lyrics that say; "Wish you were here".

The song pulls the detective into deep thought; *Where are you? If something happens to you.* The detective sighs; *Vicky,* I'll be totally lost without you. I love you so much."

Inside the diner Patricia fills patron's cups with coffee.

A man reaches up to the television and turns the volume up as high as it can go.

He then shouts, "Be quiet!"

"This is a Channel Six News Update. Hello this is Lou Trudeau. There're many law officers looking for the ones who are responsible. They all have one goal, to protect us and keep us safe. Let them do their job and keep your eyes open for anything suspicious. Tonight, I am here inside the lobby of theater waiting for the movie to end. Will the movie live up to all the hype? So far, the only ones that I have talked to are the ushers. They've informed me that a few patrons had to be removed from the theater for shouting out profanities. Here come some people leaving now. Excuse me, how was the movie?"

Several teenagers walk by with their thumbs pointing down. One of the prancing young men shout. "This theater, this town and the movie suck. They should give us our money back."

A young girl stops for the camera. "It's boring because it's about the victim's lives, their dreams and the neighborhood they grew up in. It sucked really bad. It was nothing like the book."

Hearing the response, the diner gets loud with chatter.

Patricia goes into the kitchen and says to the cook. "I got to take a break. I'm going out back to smoke a blunt. If anyone wants to take a hit of this mind shredder bud, I'll be out back." Patricia puts on a coat, walks through the kitchen and out the back door. She takes refuge from the blowing snow between the dumpster and the building. She lights up. Hearing a buzzing sound, she looks up to see a drone flying overhead. She puffs and blows smoke up towards the drone.

Hidden within the darkness behind the dumpster is a crouching woman.

Her insidious thoughts close in on her sanity; "Patricia you always take your break at this time. Lloyd and Ida should be on their way home and soon will be getting ready for bed. You're all slaves to your routines. It's like clockwork." Numbing reality her thoughts poison her mind; "I am invisible. But very soon everyone will know who I am. They'll see that I am here to do God's will. Now it's time for this whore to meet her maker!" Euphorically she gleefully surrenders to her darkest inner demon's blood lust. "Oh, let's not forget our little sister and her big show. Yes, another piece of the Master's plan."

Leaning her head back looking up at the drone Patricia blows out another puff of smoke; *I'm as stoned as a goat. I wonder if they can see me. But I am glad I have someone to cover for me while I go over to the lodge to see Lexis's new routine. I know Jennifer is going to be busy tonight. I guess I'll have help her out.*

The back door of the diner opens and a man wearing an apron yells into the wind, "Boss, you're wanted in here."

Patricia sighs and yells back. "What now."

"Table six says they want to see the owner."

"Tell them I'm in the bathroom."

Patricia puts the blunt to her lips and takes a slow easy draw. She coughs, raises the blunt up towards the drone, "Want a hit?"

Inside the police department the Taskforce Commander puts his phone to his ear, "Hello, this is Agent Mahoney, are you in charge of aerial surveillance?"

A woman's voice answers and says. "Yes sir. We're watching live feeds from the drones as we speak. We have sky views from over the theater and lodge. We also launched three quadcopters. One is over the diner and two are covering streets that lead in and out of the Moon Lake area."

Agent Mahoney says, "I want to keep an eye on longtime residents who are by themselves. Use the quadcopters that are covering the streets."

"We won't have to do that. We are putting two more quad-copters in the sky right now. We have the potential victim list and so we will focus on tracking them."

The Taskforce Commander replies, "Good job. You guys are way ahead of me. Are those quadcopters equipped with night vision and thermal cameras?"

"Yes, all the drones are."

"Great. And so, when the movie lets out, I need a sky views over Hanson Manor and the Lodge."

"Yes sir." The woman then hangs up the phone and continues to watch the several video feeds on the computer screen. She then notices movement of a thermal image behind the dumpster of the diner. Realizing it is slowly moving towards Patricia her heart races. The woman shouts. "Someone's behind the dumpster. Their getting ready to attack Patricia!"

Anticipation

Inside the theater the audience watches the last scene play out on the movie screen. With the Unicorn Theater in the foreground a group of laughing teenagers walk toword it. They talk about their aspirations and dreams. Approaching the theater, they fade into nothingness. The silence in the theater is broken by the people in attendance clapping, cheering and whistling. The movie credits roll down the screen and the lights of the theater go on.

Richard gets up out if his chair and wipes tears from his eyes and says, "Hey Jude, what did you think?"

With tears in her eyes she replies, "They came alive. It felt like they were right here with me. I loved it."

Lexis says, "I thought it was great. I'm glad they kicked out the kids who were yelling." She looks at Judy and then says, "If you guys want to go to the party, I can drop you off. I just want to get to the lodge and watch the competition." Lexis looks at Dean and sees him wiping tears from his eyes. "Papa. what about you?"

"Kelly and I have to go to the premier party. But we'll be at the lodge for your performance. So, I will see all of you later."

Visibly shaken Dean gets up, along with his date clutching his arm and they step into the isle. While they walk up the isle people congratulate them on the movie.

Lloyd says to Lexis, "We're not going anywhere until this crowd clears. Then we will meet you at the car."

Ida takes hold of Lloyd's hand, "Yes, it's past Lloyd's bed time. But it was such a wonderful movie."

Judy smiles, "It got me to remember how close Shannon and her friends were. They loved being together."

Ida pats Lloyd's hand, "Lloyd would get furious when they would knock at our door and run off."

Lloyd then says, "It was in the middle of the night. Anyone would get mad."

Richard says, "I'll meet you guys at the car. I'm going upstairs to see if they need any more help." He kisses Judy and says to her, "Are you going to be okay?"

"I have the rest of my life to morn for Tommy."

Richard steps out into the isle and disappears into the crowd.

Judy says, "I have some things to do before I go. Wait here and then we'll all walk out together."

"Can I come with?" Lexis asks.

Sure Lex, I just have to clean up a little and thank the ushers for helping out."

Before Judy and Lexis walk away Judy reminds Ida and Lloyd that she will be right back.

Yawning Lloyd looks at Ida, "I can barely keep my eyes open."

Ida says, "The movie got me thinking. Do you remember when we first got Shannon? How she uses to talk about a sister named Elizabeth."

"Yes, but the psychologist said that it most likely an imaginary friend. And when she got older, she never mentioned it."

"No Lloyd. About a week before she was murdered, she brought up Elizabeth. She said she didn't know why she believed that she had a sister. She said that she didn't remember anything before she came to live with us. Shannon was really frustrated that she could not remember anything about her childhood. She also said that she always wondered who her real parents were."

Hopes and Dreamscapes

Gildardo turns to Martha and he reaches out for her. With every ounce of energy, she reaches out to take hold of his hand. Within her mind she fights for this vision not to fade. Regaining coconsciousness, she feels snowflakes melting on her face. Hearing the cold wind howl Martha opens her eyes. She then rolls over onto her back. Sprawled out on the frozen lake she gazes up at the snowflakes falling from the night sky. She feels a sharp pain on the top of her head. After rubbing it she looks at her hand. Seeing blood, her stomach becomes queasy.

She thinks to herself; *Where am I? Where's Gildardo?*

She tries to calm herself by letting her mind go blank and taking a deep breath.

After a few minutes she feels confident to stand up.

"Oh my God. I remember. There's the lodge. I have to make it there."

Fearing for her life, she stumbles toward the lodge.

Within her mind she pleads; *Help me God! Please watch over us and give us strength.*

Staggering across the frozen lake, Martha's face and hands are numb. She tries to block out the stinging pain by concentrating on the blinking lights.

Zongzi's eyes come in focus. He finds himself embedded underneath the surface of the frozen lake. Stunned he looks up through the ice. He sees the green and blue lights streak across the moonlit sky.

Shaking in shock Zongzi ponders; *I'm freezing! I was more comfortable inside the fish.*

Still looking up through the ice, Zongzi concentrates to relax. He allows this calmness to fill his spirit. Seeping into his conscious mind he begins to hear approaching footsteps. He then sees the bottom of boots step overhead and across the ice.

Zongzi breathes deeps and thinks; *The challenges in life are a gift to strengthen the soul.* He exhales slowly. *By helping others, you help yourself.*

With these words Zongzi's spirit passes up through the ice. Floating in the moonlight above lake he hears can feel the wind. He also feels the snowflakes land and melt on his face. Happy to be alive he is not disturbed by the freezing temperature. Determined to help, he follows the woman. His eyes grow wide noticing the blood dripping from her head.

He can hear her thoughts; *I wonder if that man is coming after me? Please God let don't let him catch me.*

Zongzi then looks around and spots someone who is following her.

Knowing that her life is in danger, he thinks; *I am here for a reason.*

Floating in midair he continues to watch over her. Zongzi cringes realizing that a man is going to catch up to her. The presence of evil is palpable. He studies the man and what he's wearing. Looking even closer he sees hideous spirits riding on the back of the large man. Their hateful eyes glare at him.

In unison the demonic voices shriek, "We see you Zongzi. Welcome into our world."

The demons then jump onto Zongzi. They scream in ecstasy biting and clawing into his spirit. Zongzi fights back and tries desperately to keep his eyes on the woman.

Still staggering across the lake Martha looks behind her and sees the man.

She then looks up to the sky and screams, "God help me!"

Hearing the woman's plea, Zongzi pushes the vicious fiends off his face. He then sees a man running toward the woman. The man grabs her by the hair. Fighting with fury Martha swings wildly. The man quickly puts her in a headlock. His arm squeezes tight around her neck until her body goes limp. After tossing the body over his shoulder he slowly scans the area.

Floating overhead Zongzi continues to fight off the demonic fiends. The dark figures squeal like swine while they rip and tear his soul.

Whispering in his sleep, Zongzi says, "That's the Strangler! To be able to stop this madman I have to wake up now. Sandy, I seen his face. The potion worked. All I have to do is wake up!"

Feeling helpless he watches the woman being carried away. Zongzi thinks; *It feels like something's happening to me. Theses demons are erasing my will to go on!*

Again, fighting to see what is happening, Zongzi catches a glimpse of the man and woman disappearing into the swirling snow.

Approaching Zongzi's room Sandy turns to Detective Sentieri, "Please be quiet and turn your phone on vibrate."

Sandy then opens the door and walks into the room. She sees Zongzi lying in bed and walks closer.

The detective then walks into the room and shuts the door.

The door closes with a bang and the detective whispers, "Sorry I didn't mean to do that."

Seeing Zongzi flinch she sits on the bed next to him. Hearing him grinding his teeth she starts to breathe deep.

Sandy thinks; *To calm him, I must be calm myself.*

In Zongzi's mind lightning bolts shatter the moonlit sky. A very loud thunderclap follows that shakes the demons off his spirit. Everything goes black and he gasps for air.

Seeing Zongzi choking, Sandy turns to the detective and points to the dresser.

"Hand me that corkscrew."

The detective quickly hands her the corkscrew. Sandy puts it on the bedside table by a green bottle. She then turns back to Zongzi and pinches the skin over his heart. Twisting the skin she softly blows at his face. Almost instantly, Zongzi stops choking and begins to snore.

Witnessing this, the detective scratches his head and thinks; *What just happened?* Feeling his phone buzz, he then quietly opens the door and steps into the hallway.

Detective Sentieri looks at the incoming phone number and answers the call.

"What's up Jack?"

"We may have caught a break. Thermal imaging from one of our drones spotted someone stalking Patricia, the owner of the diner. We have officers on the way."

"Thanks for the heads up. Anything else?"

"The movie is over and we're following potential victims. The director of the FBI wants an update and I'll be busy for a little while. If there's any developments call me."

The detective hangs up the phone, quietly opens the door to Zongzi's room and whispers, "Got to go."

After quietly shutting the door the detective steps briskly down the hallway.

Gazing out the window of the limousine, a woman sitting next to Dean wipes a tear from the corner of his eye.

"So, did the movie tell the story you wanted?"

"Yes, you're an amazing actress. You're going to win a lot of awards for your portrayal of Janis."

"I bet you didn't tell them that it was your idea to keep the violence out and focus on the lives of the victims?" She then takes hold of Dean's hand and caresses it. "Dean, you're a very good man. It was really nice getting to know you while making this film. I've learned a lot from you and what's important to have in a relationship. I've been leaning on you ever since we've met. So, it's okay to lean on me tonight."

"Kelly, the whole time I have known you, I've seen how you put others before yourself. Your beauty runs deep." Dean puts his arm around her, "Tonight, is going to be special."

Kelly kisses him on the cheek, nestles her head close to his chest and whispers, "I love you."

Surrounded by loved ones Vicky stops asking questions about where she is. Excited just to be there she fills the moment with embraces. Full of energy her trivial earthy restraints vanish. Playful and content her blissful essence shines through her eyes and she says, "It's like coming home for the holidays. Seeing loved ones and meeting relatives I've never met before. I couldn't be happier."

Seeing her sister's look of concern Vicky's peaceful emotions fade. The heavenly vibrant visions slowly disappear.

Regaining consciousness, she finds herself lying on the ground in the pitch-black darkness. Her head throbs with pain. Feeling dizzy and nauseous she hears someone at the door. It creaks opens allowing the moonlight and cold wind to fill the room. Vicky sees a man throw a body to the floor.

In a threatening tone he says, "Don't worry, I'll be right back."

Hearing someone moan Vicky feels around.

"Martha is that you?"

Feeling a cold hand, she takes hold of it and says, "Martha, Martha wake up."

The woman moans in pain and replies, "Vicky what will we do now. I don't want to die. My baby needs me."

Vicky rubs Martha's hands. "You're freezing. We have to warm you up."

"Thank you for giving me the chance to escape. The last thing I remember was running to the lights of the lodge. Are you okay?"

Vicky replies. "I think I died and went to heaven."

"What?"

"I don't know if it was a dream or not. I saw my sister who died of cancer."

"Did you see my husband?"

"No. But, it seemed so real."

Hearing footsteps coming from outside the door Martha is terror-stricken and she whispers, "What are we going to do now?"

"We're going to try again."

Sitting quietly, they hear a door open but it is not the door to the room where they are at. Soon afterward they hear a blood curdling scream of a terrified woman.

Fixations

With her eyes on the computer screen the bespectacled woman says. "Just got off the phone with the Agent Mahoney. He told me that Agents should be at the diner any second."
A man dressed in a gray suit walks into the cubicle and looks at the computer screen. "They're not going to make it in time. Looks like the stalker making their move."
The woman replies, "I'll fly down closer to the dumpster."
"Good idea. The drone might scare them off."
"Patricia sees us. We're not scaring her. She's blowing smoke up at us."
"Suspect's closing in." The man reaches over the woman and points to the screen. "What's that a knife?"
"No that's a cleaver." the woman quickly replies.
To get a better view of the computer screen the man pulls over a chair and sits beside the woman.
"Dive and crash into the stalker." Reacting to what he's sees he then says distressingly, "Oh no."
At the lodge a man walks up to the bar, "Hey bartender can you bring me some more fish?"
Salting a pile of hot french-fries Jennifer says, "Just give me a second."
She then puts down the saltshaker and brings a plate of fish over to the man.
He thanks her with a ten-dollar tip and points to a crowd entering the lodge, "The movie must be over."
Jennifer waves the incoming patrons over to the bar. After hanging up their coats they walk over to the bar and sit down. "How was the movie?" Jennifer asks.
With a look of amazement one of the women replies, "The storyline was captivating. The dialogue heartfelt and the acting was surreal."
"I guess you liked it. So, what can I get for you?"
"We're waiting for the rest of our group. But we would like to have some drinks?"
"What would you like."
Randy walks up and says, "Excuse me ladies."

He then whispers in his wife's ear. "Dean called and said that Kelly and him will be here for Lexis's performance."

Excited Jennifer turns and looks at him. "Did they give you a time?"

"He said in about an hour."

Servicing the patrons at the bar Jennifer thinks; *I wonder if the whole cast is coming here. Wow, I can't believe all this is happening. I hope Judy's doing okay. With her brother being murdered, she is going to be a mess. Tommy had such a big heart. If she does not call soon, I'm going to call her.*

Seeing sweat gathering on Zongzi's brow Sandy gets a hand towel from the bathroom and wipes it off. She then quickly opens a bottle of wine, lifts his head up and pours some of it into his mouth. After he swallows down the wine, Sandy lies his head back down onto the pillow. She then pulls up a chair and sits down to watch over him.

Taking deep breaths, she closes her eyes.

She then opens her hands over his body, "May you be filled with peace. Follow your consciousness into the root of your being. Be immersed within the purity of the love."

She sways in deep meditation before she opens her eyes. She raises one of Zongzi's eyelids and sees that his eye is jerking back and forth, side to side.

In that moment Zongzi's spirit is invigorated with wonder. The wind lifts him higher up into the sky. He then looks down to the icy lake glistening in the moonlight. Euphoria captures his thoughts and entices him into a frozen daze. With his mouth open in awe he watches the snowflakes circle in the wind. In the distance he then hears a church bell ring.

Trying to recapture his thoughts Zongzi counts the bell as it rings. *One, two, three, four, five, six, seven. Why does that seem to be important? Why do I feel so uneasy about what time it is?*

Floating there in midair Zongzi opens his heart. He looks around and realizes that he is in a dreamscape.

I am in a dream. But why am I here?

He begins to recognize the surroundings and sees blinking lights.

Now I remember. That's the lodge across the lake. It's where I am staying. Tonight, at nine o'clock they're having a talent contest. It's all coming back to me now. This is Moon Lake. I'm here to find out who the killer is. Now I remember. I just seen a man carrying a woman away. Where did he go? Where did he take the woman?

Trying to soothe the deep urgency he puts his spirit at ease. He relaxes his mind and breathes in slowly through his nose. This lowers him to the ground and he then begins to search the area for clues.

Sensing misery in the air Zongzi follows the scent like a bloodhound. Spotting a trail of footsteps in the snow he begins to run. *Faster! I must get there as fast as I can.* He darts along the lakeshore, up and over the embankment. He then follows the footprints down to a cellar door.

Seeing the door open Zongzi stops and sees a man walks out. *I recognize him. He wasn't wearing glasses when I saw him out on the lake. But I do remember that gray coat. That's the killer! I know it is. I can feel it. What's he holding? Shoestrings!* The man locks the door behind him and walks up the stairs. A suffocating egocentric introspective engulfs the heartless man with self-importance.

Giggling, he whispers, "Got to tie up a couple loose ends. Hope she didn't start without me. Yes, Ida and Lloyd are the icing on the cake."

Seeing the man disappear into the windblown snow, Zongzi rushes down into the cellar. He comes to a door and tries to open it. But it is locked and he cannot turn the door handle.

Execution

Standing outside their home Ida and Lloyd wave goodbye as Lexis's car drives away.

Lloyd opens the door for Ida and says, "If I ever get a chance, I'm going to shoot the killer right in the head. No, I take that back. That's too quick. I want that murderer to suffer. Maybe pour boiling water over their head. Then cool them off by throwing them outside in the freezing cold. Let them freeze to death!"

Ida gives her husband a displeasing look and says, "Please stop saying things like that.

Closing the door behind them, Lloyd helps his wife with her coat and hangs it up. After hanging up his coat he joins his wife in the kitchen.

"I can't relax. I am so furious knowing that the person who killed my daughter is still out there."

Ida walks over to the pots and pans stacked up by the sink. Lloyd then says, "Honey I'll do the dishes tomorrow."

Ida does not reply and begins to scrub a skillet in the sink, "I don't want to hear anymore from you tonight. You're making me sick to my stomach."

Lloyd raises his arms over his head, "Can't I speak my mind in my own house? Please honey sit down. I'll do the dishes tomorrow."

"No." Ida points at her husband and says, "You take a seat. This is my house too. After seeing that movie my heart is breaking too. We should be at the lodge supporting Lexis!"

Lloyd takes a deep breath and sits down at the table.

He rubs his forehead and says, "You're right."

Ida turns and looks at Lloyd, "Do you really mean that? She would be so happy to see us there."

Behind Lloyd, a woman leaps out of the closet and screams, "You're not going anywhere!"

Harboring pathetic delusions of saintliness, the woman covers Lloyd's face with a chloroformed soaked cloth. He struggles and trys to break free. Unable to stay conscious Lloyd's body hits the floor with a thud. Numb with fright Ida's voce shakes belting out a shrill scream.

Deeply rooted in the attacker's mind self-named revengeful thoughts blossom. Surfacing from the abyss of dementia like maggots they bore deeper into the pith of the woman. Uncensored ramblings mutate into actions as she prepares to unveil her blood thirsty debauchery.

With wide eyes drenched in turmoil, the possessed woman points at Ida, "Now it's your turn!"

Ida throws her hands up in the air and darts out of the kitchen. Clutching a clever in hand and laughing manically the deranged woman chases after her.

Floating above the clouds an exhilarating buzz fills Zongzi's spirit. He passes over land and sea. Like a pinwheel he is blown carelessly father and father from the earth. Riding on solar winds, stars flash by drifting deeper into the cosmos. Shades of orange and yellow wash over his mind. Pink, purple and gold wash over his consciousness. Hues of green and blue swirl around him as his thoughts fade into nothingness.

Sensing the urgency of the moment Sandy searches for a pulse. Trying to hear his heart beat she puts her head on Zongzi's chest. Instantly she then pounds her fist on his chest. Sandy breathes deep, pinches his nose and blows air into his mouth. Trying to revive him she put one hand over the other and pushes down on his chest.

Tears roll down her face. In desperation, she slaps him across the face and shouts, "You are not going to leave me!" Sandy then hugs Zongzi as tight as she can, "I will never forgive myself for doing this to you!"

Screaming like a banshee the cleaver welding woman chases Ida around the house. Ida runs into Shannon's room and shuts the door behind her. She puts her shoulder against it and tries to keep the woman from pushing the door open. The woman easily pushes the door open and the elderly woman falls backward to the floor. The disheveled woman steps into the room. She towers over Ida and glares at her with her unsettling, maniacal eyes.

Petrified, Ida realizes the attacker resemblance to her deceased daughter. "Elisabeth is that you!"

Breathing heavily the assailant pauses and looks around the room. She sees pictures of Shannon and her sunny face. Catching her breath, a calmness washes over the savage intruder.

Sitting at the bar a man waves to Jennifer, "I'll have another drink. And, can you turn off the television?"

"I'll get you a drink. But I can't turn off the newscast because everyone's watching it." Jennifer replies.

Displeased the man sighs.

On television, the camera closes in on the face of the newscaster as he says, "Dr. Strumpell, can you revive the mental deficiencies of the criminal mind?"

The camera switches to the distinguished, bearded psychologist sitting in a burgundy, button tufted chair.

The astute gentleman replies, "Cognitive science, the study of behavior and mental processes is evolving. We strive to understand conscious and unconscious relationships to our behavior. By way of measuring and evaluation of a subject's response we seek an understanding of the emergent properties of the brain. To diagnose and treat mental processes is an ongoing daunting task. Our efforts to combat psychological disturbances that have taken root deep into the subconscious is our objective. These disturbances are like a cancer that feeds on healthy mental processes. Mitigating improper synapses is a complex process. They are also simplistic solutions and remedies. To put it simplistically, you can lead a horse to water but you can't make them drink. In most cases the mental storm is self-perpetuating. The short answer to your question is yes. However, unraveling complex mental thought processes may sound plausible in theory. To diagnose and treat is a whole new ball of wax."

Overwhelmed with her own thoughts Jennifer reaches for her phone; *I have to call Judy.*

"Hello, just seeing if you need anything?"

"Thanks for calling Jennifer. We're on our way. Is there a lot of people there?"

"The place is filling up quick."

Richard realizes that Judy is talking to Jennifer and he nudges his wife.

Judy acknowledges her husband request and says, "Richard wants to reserve a table close to the stage."

"Of course, we'll reserve a table."

Driving down the snowy street Detective Sentieri thinks; *It's a quarter to eight.*

Looking down the street he then sees police cars with red flashing lights behind the diner.

"Well, it's almost eight and looks like I'm too late." Hearing his phone, the detective activates the call and says, "What's up Jack?"

"The full DNA report came back. Two separate DNA sequences were recovered from the Theater and Chicago crime scenes. Both share a genetic marker. So, the killers are biologically related. The DNA clears Lexis and Dean. But they also share this genetic marker. Meaning that they are biologically related to the killers."

The detective's phone alerts him that he has another phone call and Rob quickly says, "Okay Jack, thanks for the information. I've got another call."

The detective stops his car and begins to turn around as he activates the other call.

A woman voice says, "Detective Sentieri, Ida and Lloyd are in danger. You got to get there as fast as you can."

"Is this Sandy Adams?"

"Yes. Please hurry. Zongzi also told me that the killer abducted a woman and carried her into a cellar. The house is directly across the lake from the lodge. You have to hurry!"

The indecisiveness of the assailant gives way to callousness. Pent-up rage fuels her unwarranted mayhem.

Laughing hysterically the insidious woman walks closer to Ida. She raises the cleaver high in the air and says calmly, "God, give me strength to glorify You."

Ida throws up her hands to shield her head and shrieks. From behind the intruder, a black iron skillet whacks the crazed woman in the back of head. Ida watches the woman fall to the ground. She then sees her husband standing there holding the skillet.

Noticing a shadowy figure approaching him from behind, her eyes fill with terror and she shouts, "Look out!"

Spinning his tiers in the snow the detective pulls up to Ida and Lloyd's house. He rushes into the front door. Hearing someone scream he runs down the hallway. Coming to a room he sees Lloyd struggling with a man. Lloyd breaks free and slugs the man in the face. The man's round spectacles fall onto the ground.

Lloyd rushes over to his wife and holds her. "Are you okay?"

Detective Sentieri pulls out his gun and points it at the man. "The gigs up."

The man sneers at the detective and points at the clock on the wall. "Looks like you blew it again Robbie."

The detective looks a clock on the wall and sees that it is eight o'clock. Dreadful thoughts flash in the detective's mind.

Regaining consciousness from the blow to the head the deranged woman gets to her feet. From behind, she creeps up on the detective and swings the cleaver at his head. Off in the distance a loud explosion is heard. The explosion disrupts woman's aim and the cleaver catches nothing but air.

Dean then rushes into the room and grabs a hold of the woman. He struggles with her and forces her to drop the cleaver.

Moments later, Police officers' storm into the house. They place handcuffs on the man and the disheveled woman. The two try to resist but the officers take then into custody.

Being escorted out the door, the handcuffed man shouts. "Moon Lake would be nothing without me. You all owe me." The man looks at Detective Sentieri and says. "I am the most infamous serial killer of all time!"

Ida responds. "May God have mercy on your soul."

With the killers inside the squad car, Dean's date runs to him. Detective Sentieri joins them on the front lawn. Dean tells the detective that Lexis is in the Limousine and that they are on their way to the Lodge.

Interrupting their conversation, the detective's phone rings He then answers the phone, "Tell me what happened Jack."

"Someone wants to say hi." the Taskforce Commander replies.

"Hi dad. It's me, your long-lost daughter who has come home."

Looking upward the detective replies. "Lori, where have you've been? And you're grounded."

The killers had me locked in a room and they told me about the bomb. But just minutes before it went off the wind blew the door open. Hold on dad there's someone else who wants to talk to you."

"Honey! It was the strangest thing. The wind blew the door open just before the house blew up. Martha and I are both okay. She went home but I have nowhere to go. Any ideas?"

Later that night, Detective Sentieri and Vicky embrace tenderly in the pantry of the lodge.

The detective whispers in her ear. "Are you sure you're okay?"

"I'm in your arms, I'm okay."

"Where's Lori?"

"She took Bonkers up to her room and she said she'll be back down in a few minutes."

At the bar Jennifer serves Sandy, Zongzi and Patricia a pitcher of beer. Ida, Lloyd and Judy sit at a table close to the stage. Across the table Dean, his date and Richard raise their glasses for a toast.

Richard says, "To unforgettable memories we'll cherish forever."

Together they all take a drink and then turn their attention to the stage where Lexis is about to perform.

The end.

"Thank you for reading the Shoestring Strangler." Rick Sentieri

Made in the USA
Monee, IL
02 July 2021

71975346R00100